MW01233778

*Bryan M. Powell*

# The Oath

*Bryan M. Powell*

# The Oath

*Bryan M. Powell*

Suspense - Fiction, Christian - Fiction, Young Adult – Fiction, Political - Fiction
Cover design by Steve Wright at wrightsteve@25
Photography by Amy McCarthy –
photographybymccarthy@gmail.com
Manufactured in the United States of America
ISBN-13: 978-1-5464-3520-4
ISBN-10: 1-5464-3520-4

# Endorsement

While reading this story, I was blown away how real and 3D all the characters, scenes, and events are. I felt like I was on Air Force One, in the speeding car toward freedom, and could see the gunshots and explosions as they unfolded throughout. The Bible verses were extra credit helpers in understanding the story better as well. If you never have heard of Bryan Powell before, after reading these books, you will never forget him. You can also read this book and enjoy it even if you've never read the first one. I give this book five out of five stars because I believe readers have another great thriller/suspense writer to escape with like Joel Rosenberg, Ted Dekker, and Frank Peretti.

Bradley Evans,
writer/reviewer for books and movies
music2movies@yahoo.com

The Oath is an exciting, multifaceted, suspenseful drama. The diabolical plot and extent of deception is captivating. It compels continuous reading to follow the pursuits of the main characters on their mission; enlisting the reader to be accomplice and a cheering participant. The author, Bryan M. Powell, weaves terror, emotion, ingenuity, stealth, bravery, heroism, and faith with determined resolve in this fast paced series of crucial and eventful exploits … A riveting message, inspirational, and rewarding.

William (Bill) G. Billups,
Chief Warrant Officer (CWO2),
United States Navy (Retired)

# Caveat

In the spirit of full disclosure, I must admit this is the second edition of the Stranger in the White House. Having written 13 novels since this book, I have learned a few things and attempted to bring them into play in this story. I hope you enjoy it.

# Dedication

To my patient and supportive wife, Patty, who has waited up for me more nights than I can count, and to my granddaughters, Reagan and Madison, who kept asking for the next book in the series.

To my many first readers, Brad, Courtney, and Eileen, who have saved my bacon on more than one occasion with their helpful critiques.

To my editor(s) at Tate Publishing and all those up and down the line who have worked tirelessly to get this book out in time. And especially to the Lord; without Him, I could do nothing. We are indeed co-laborers in the task of spreading the gospel through stories. He is the author and finisher of my faith; I am His ready scribe.

# Character Biographies

Chase Newton – investigative reporter with the New York Times, Washington, D.C. branch and the only man that Vice President Randall could trust with his life.

Megan Newton – Chase's wife, the woman in the eye of the storm.

Stan Berkowitz – editor in chief of the New York Times, Washington, D.C. branch, a tough no nonsense editor that got too close to the truth.

President James F. Randall – President of the United States of America, a man with a questionable past and future.

Senator Max Wilcox – the President's choice for the next Vice President, someone with connections.

Vice President Randall – the current Vice President, a hunted man. Glenn Tibbits – retired CIA agent who kept a file on everyone.

Sheriff Conyers – the Sheriff of Beaumont, Colorado who was in the right place at the right time.

Dr. Cleve Newberry – chief medical attendant to the President who had an important role to play and played it well.

Nurse Hodges – Dr. Newberry's assistant wasn't who she said she was.

Nguyen (Wynn) Xhu – first generation immigrant from Vietnam, was chosen to be the temporary Chief of Staff, a determined woman with one mission to fulfill.

The Dean – a man with a long shadow and a sordid past.

# Prologue

**Air Force One ...**

Vice President Randall stood before Judge Patricia Fisher, of the 6th Circuit Court of Appeals, raised his right hand and with an even tone, recited the thirty-nine words that make a common citizen the next President of the United States of America.

"I do solemnly swear that I will faithfully execute the office of President of the United States, and will to the best of my ability, preserve, protect and defend the Constitution of the United States so help me God."

He smiled, shook hands with the judge, and turned to the small group of cameramen and reporters gathered in the airborne Oval Office.

President Randall took his place behind a small podium and spoke without the benefit of a teleprompter with a steady voice. "Today we have once again seen tragedy strike at the heart of our nation. And though sadly, it may have hit its head, it missed its heart; for you, my fellow Americans, are the heart of this great land. You are the life-force that keeps this country alive and well and free. It is this kind of determination and resolve that you demonstrate every day when you get up and go to the factories and fields of this great country those who would seek to do us harm can never destroy. It is that kind of energy, that kind of drive, that yearning to be free that will guide us through these dark days.

So it is with sadness and with joy I stand before you today to lead you out of the malaise of the past unto a brighter tomorrow. Together we will close the chapter on the past and move forward to a future filled with hope and promise, a future filled with freedom and justice for all, and a future where our children's children will live in peace with all mankind." Then he looked directly into the lens of the camera with his steel gray eyes as if he were looking into the very soul of the nation. "And we will not rest until we see that day dawn on the horizon of an earth that had been reborn. I ask you join me on this journey." The 47th president concluded his brief remarks, did an about face, closed his eyes and prayed to the voice inside his head.

The voice answered, "A new day is about to dawn, but it isn't the one these poor fools dream of." A wicked grin parted his lips, which he quickly suppressed.

# Chapter One

It was a cold, rainy Monday afternoon in April and all the residents of Washington, D.C., along with the nation, wanted to do was mourn the passing of a great man.

Chase Newton, a gifted investigative correspondent with *The New York Times,* sat staring out of his corner office window as the rain beat against the glass. The thoughts of the day's tragic events passed before his eyes like a 'B' rated movie.

His rise to fame came as the result of his investigation of The Order less than two years ago. As a cub reporter with *The Beaumont Observer,* he'd gone underground and discovered The Order was a clandestine organization whose stated goal was the destruction of America. He not only saved America from a disastrous chapter in her life, but his heroic efforts resulted in his life taking a major turn for the better.

His office, located on the floor of the Willard Building on G Street, was not far from the White House. Awards lined the walls of his palatial office. There were pictures of him and the President of the United States shaking hands, a picture of him and the governor of Colorado, and a plaque displaying his Pulitzer Prize for Investigative Journalism. There were many other awards and Certificates lining his walls, but the one photograph that he was most proud was of him and Megan on their wedding day.

After all of the interviews, the sworn testimonies before House and Senate sub-committees, and hearings before the House Rules on Ethics, life, as an investigative reporter, returned to normal. That is, as normal as it could be commuting between New York, Washington, D.C. and Beaumont, Colorado. It was during the intense undercover operation in which he had placed himself in harm's way to uncover the plot of The Order that he realized he was madly in love with Megan Richards. Megan, or M, as Chase affectionately called her, is the daughter of T. J. Richards, the pastor of the now defunct Community First Church of Beaumont and leader of The Order. His disappearance was a mystery yet to be solved, only then could he really celebrate. But today was not a day for celebration.

Chase's life was about to take another turn.

The annoying buzz of his telephone jolted Chase from his musings. It was a back line, one that circumvented the secretary pool. He lifted the phone from its cradle and listened.

"Chase, listen to me, the man who was sworn into the office of the presidency an hour ago is an impostor."

The one speaking to Chase was one he knew well ... it was the voice of the vice president.

An hour earlier a violent attack had taken place against the government. Insurgents plotted and carried out a plan to kill the president. They succeeded.

President Richard C. Donovan the 46th president had only been in office one term and had successfully won reelection. His second term was in its third year when he was tragically cut down. As designated by the Constitution, the line of succession called for the immediate confirmation of the vice president to the office of the presidency.

*How could he be an impostor?* Chase tried to digest this information. He knew the vice president well. He had interviewed him on several occasions and they had become good friends. How could someone other than the vice president be sworn into the office of the presidency without the Secret Service, the FBI, and the press not knowing about it? And who is this on the phone telling this outrageous story? Questions flew around Chases' mind like bats in a cave. This was turning into a living nightmare.

"What is today's password?" Chase asked the caller.

Only a few knew the daily password, but because Chase was in the press corps and received daily briefings, he knew what it was.

"Today's password is 'cakewalk' now listen Chase, there was not only a successful attack against the president, there was an attempt on my life as well. Obviously, they failed, or I wouldn't be speaking to you. But they think I'm dead, and someone who looks just like me, was sworn in as the president of the United States. When they discover I'm still alive, my life won't last five minutes. I've got to go into hiding and you have got to expose this plot to take over our government," the vice president's voice grew thick with emotion.

Sweat beaded on Chase's upper lip as he tried to absorb the import of what the vice president had said. "It's The Order again isn't it?"

The vice president let a moment pass before answering. "I don't know about that Son, I just know whoever did it, knew both our itineraries and knew the best time to hit us," he said through clinched teeth.

Chase stiffened in his seat, his mind was swirling. "Did anyone see it? Were there any eyewitnesses?" he asked as he ran his fingers through his hair.

The momentary pause seemed to stretch into an hour as Chase waited for the vice president to speak.

"Yes there were, but sadly they were eliminated too. None of my security detail survived the attack." His voice rang hollow, emotionally spent.

"How is it that you survived Mr. Vice President?" Chase pressed, as he took out a note pad and started scribbling franticly.

The vice president's voice turned conspiratorial. "I'll get to that in a moment, but suffice it to say, it won't be long before they learn that I am still alive."

"Well what can I do Mr. Vice President?"

Another pause held Chase's attention.

"Once I am secure, I will call and give you as much information as I can, but for now I have got to go." The telephone conversation ended as suddenly as it started.

# Chapter Two

hase sat stunned as he mulled over his options. *The New York Times,* Washington Bureau, was not the place to spawn a major scandal, and this certainly had the makings of one. Where do you begin an investigation of a sitting president? The question haunted Chase as he stared out his window. Should I walk into the Oval Office and say 'Mr. President, you are an impostor'? No, that would only get me arrested and put behind bars for a very long time. I need to get some help, but who? Who can I trust with the biggest story in the country and not blow it before I could corroborate it?

The only man he could trust was his friend and editor, Stan Berkowitz. Not only did Chase benefit greatly from uncovering a plot to take over the country, but so did Stan. As editor of *The Beaumont Observer,* Stan was credited with having the savvy to know a big story when he saw one. As the result of his involvement in the undercover investigation, Stan was immediately promoted by *The New York Times* to Editor and Chief of the Washington, D.C. bureau.

His enviable position placed him under a lot of pressure, which he shared with his reporters. He demanded the facts before the hype. As was true of him in Beaumont, so it was true of him now, he had a way of driving his reporters to new heights, or new depths, depending on your perspective. Despite his new position, his personality hadn't changed either, he was still just as crusty as he ever was.

There was one other thing that had not changed about Stan, if he thought that you were on to a big story, all the resources of the paper were behind you. Chase needed Stan and he needed those resources now.

Chase, dressed in a golf shirt and slacks, stepped off of the elevator on the fourteenth floor and charged down the wide corridor and entered Stan's Office.

Giving little heed to the women in the secretary pool, he headed straight for the door to the newspaper's headquarters. With a jerk, he pulled it open and stepped inside. Still breathing hard, he was met with the cold stare of Stan's personal secretary, Mrs. Hudson.

"Hello Mr. Newton, are you here to see Mr. Berkowitz?" Chase had not gotten used to all this formality, but he humored her by answering her question.

Chase nodded. "Yes, Ma'am."

She looked over her glasses. "Do you have an appointment?" she inquired.

"No, Ma'am, but—"

Cutting him off with an icy glare, Mrs. Hudson cleared her throat and addressed Chase like a kindergarten teacher would an unruly child.

"Mr. Newton, Mr. Berkowitz is a very busy man and you can't just barge in on him like you did in the old days. You're in the big league now and you have got to learn to go through the proper channels." Her condescending tone made Chase want to throttle her.

He jammed his hands in his pockets and returned a toothy smile. You must be enjoying the power of your position Mrs. Hudson.

"If he's got just a few minutes, I really need to see Stan, I mean, Mr. Berkowitz, now. It's urgent," Chase said, glancing at his Rolex watch.

Mrs. Hudson eyed him with suspicion. "Yes, well, it seems that it is always urgent with you Mr. Newton, but I'll check Mr. Berkowitz's schedule to see if I can work you in." Then she peered down at his itinerary.

Chase felt heat creeping up his neck as he waited for Mrs. Hudson to scan Mr. Berkowitz's itinerary.

"Look Ms. uh, Mrs. Hudson, if you don't let me in to see Stan in one minute, I'm going to ..."

Suddenly, the door swung open and a burst of laughter interrupted Chase before he finished his threat. Stan stepped out followed by a gentleman whom Chase had not met. The two men shook hands and parted company with the usual, 'I'll be in touch' and 'let's do lunch' type of comments and parted. With a quick nod, Stan signaled to Chase. "Come in Chase, you look like you've seen a ghost."

Mrs. Hudson's head jerked up from the appointment book, her eyes narrowing. Chase gave her a wry smile and stepped around her desk.

Once inside, it dawned on him, how much larger Stan's office was. It made Chase's look like a kid's playroom. His was the hub of all that went on in Washington, D.C. and if anyone was in the know, it was Stan.

"You look like you have seen a ghost. Chase. What's on your mind?" Stan asked as he took his seat behind his cluttered desk.

Chase hesitated, wondering if he should go out on this limb, "Stan, we've got a problem."

His face tightened. "What do you mean 'we?' You're the investigative reporter with the Pulitzer Prize hanging on your wall."

Chase sighed. "Look, Stan, can we talk freely? I mean your office isn't bugged or anything is it?" he asked, as he looked around the room.

Stan's jaw tightened. "Now Chase, you're not getting paranoid are you? You're not having flashbacks of Beaumont are you?" He replied as he crossed his arms and looked at his new Doxa watch.

With an extra effort of will-power Chase pushed himself forward. "No, Stan, I'm not paranoid, but I am worried that if what I'm about to tell you falls into the wrong hands WE both are going to be swimming at the bottom of the Potomac River."

Stan shook his head in disbelief. "That's a pretty heavy piece of information. I sure hope you have the facts to back it up before you go and get me involved," he said as he eyed

Chase wearily.

Chase put his hands of his boss's desk and leaned in closer. "You know I've got a nose for the news, but I didn't dig this up. It came to me in the form of a phone call. You see, I just got off the phone with the vice president of the United States," Chase paused to let that sink in.

Stan blinked absently. "How could you do that, the president hasn't appointed one yet?" A doubtful tone crept into his voice.

Chase shook his head. "You don't understand and I don't think I do either, but the man I just spoke to claimed to be Vice President Randall."

"You mean President Randall, don't you?" His boss retorted.

"Nope, Vice President Randall." Chase said, emphasizing every word.

Stan folded his arms across his robust chest and leaned back. "How can that be? I just watched a circuit court of appeals judge swear Vice President Randall, into the office of President on Air Force One."

"It can't be, the man I spoke to was Vice President Randall and I can prove it, Stan."

"And how can you prove that?" his eyebrows crested in a question.

Chase shifted his gaze around the room as if to see if anyone was looking and lowered his voice. "He gave me today's password, only a limited number of people have access to that kind of information, and he knew it," he said in a conspiratorial tone.

Stan took out a handkerchief and wiped his wrinkled forehead. "Okay, tell me what today's password is and I'll verify it. If you are right WE have a problem."

Grabbing a note pad, Chase scribbled two words. "Let me write it down, but don't read it out loud."

Stan turned to his computer, typed in a code and waited. A screen came up and he entered another code. He repeated this two more times before he was in the very belly of the beast. It was one of the most secure sites on the planet, and it takes a level five clearance to get into this site ... Stan had it.

"Okay, let's see that password again."

He picked up the piece of paper and looked at it over his newly acquired bi-focals. After typing the word, he tapped his fingers on the desk and waited. The monitor screen scrolled for a moment and began flashing one word in a field of black.

Chase stood and walked around and stared at the monitor screen. There it was in black and white ... 'Cakewalk.'

Stan leaned back, the lines of his forehead furrowed in concern. "Man have we got a problem. Do you know who just left my office as you barged in?"

"No, should I?" Chase asked nonchalantly.

Stan let a moment of silence pass. "It was Senator Max Wilcox, the president's pick for VP. He was here to give me an exclusive before the news broke in this afternoon's press conference."

"Stan, I got a bad feeling about this. It's like Deja Vu all over again."

Stan paused and chose his words carefully. "Why can't the real vice president just come forward and call a press conference himself and tell the whole world who he is and be done with it?" Stan asked rhetorically.

"Because Stan," Chase said as he waved his hands animatedly, "just after the successful attack on President Donovan, there was an attack on Vice President Randall. They, whoever they are, thought that they had succeeded in killing the vice president. They think that the real James F. Randall is dead and they have pulled a bait and switch on America."

"Where is James Randall now?" Stan asked, his voice getting more tense.

"The last thing he said was that he was going into hiding and that when he was in a secure place he would call me and give me any information I need to uncover this plot."

"Uh oh, here we go again," Stan said, skimming through his Rolodex for a phone number."

"Who are you gonna call? Not Ghost Busters I hope." Chase's attempt at humor fell on deaf ears.

Stan eyed Chase carefully as he picked up the phone.

"Do you remember Glenn and his daughter, what's her name, uh, Susan, no uh, Jennifer?"

Chase's eyes widened. "Yes. How could I forget? I spent hours with that woman pouring over meaningless numbers and I did it without a word of complaint," said Chase with a distant glint in his eye.

"Well those numbers weren't meaningless after all."

"I'd do it again in a heartbeat if I had to," Chase interjected.

Stan just shook his head. "Well, simmer down boy, you are a married man now," Stan said as if he had to remind Chase.

"Yes and happily married at that, but I was saying ..."

"I know what you were saying, but just don't stir up old feelings and mess up a good thing." His boss said instructively.

Chase lowered his eyes. "You are absolutely right my friend, but how can Glenn and Jennifer help us now? Didn't Glenn retire from the FBI's SI unit?"

Stan nodded and dialed a number. "Yes he did, but in this case we need someone who we can trust and who has the expertise to unravel this mess YOU got us into."

"Me?" Chase said incredulously. "How'd I do that?"

"You answered the phone didn't you?" Stan asked as he waited for Glenn to pick up.

# Chapter Three

The 3:00 p.m. press briefing held just off the Oral Office was about to begin when Chase's cell phone vibrated. Before he could answer it, the Press Secretary, a holdover from the previous administration, made the announcement that the president had arrived. "All rise. Ladies and gentlemen of the press corps, may I introduce to you the President of the United States, Mr. James F. Randall."

Everyone rose to their feet as President Randall stepped into the room and strode to the podium. "Thank you ladies and gentlemen of the press corps, you may be seated."

He paused a minute for the men and women before him to get settled. "It is my desire to act swiftly and decisively in naming my choice for the next vice president. After that, I will take a few questions." He spoke without a teleprompter.

"Today I will be submitting the name," he paused to let the cameras flash and the curiosity build, "Max Wilcox as my choice for vice president. As you know Senator Max Wilcox has been my friend and ally for many years. You will remember when I was a senator we crafted many key pieces of legislation together. Some of those never made it into law; some of them died in committee or were vetoed during the Campbell administration. With my friend Senator Max

Wilcox, soon to be Vice President Max Wilcox, at my side, we will bring these pieces of legislation back to the Senate and House and I will sign them."

Both he and the senator were liberal Democrats who looked at the Constitution as an impediment to their liberal agenda implemented. If they got their way, America would not look the same in four to eight years.

He waited for those taking notes to catch up. He was enjoying the moment.

"Now I will take a few questions from the press." He scanned the group looking for a particular hand.

The first question was a soft ball from an AP correspondent.

"Mr. President, do you think that Senator Max Wilcox will have any trouble being approved by the congress?"

President Randall knew the importance of appearing decisive and spoke in no uncertain terms.

"Mr. Wilcox is a well-respected member of the Senate and has been for the last 20 years. With the current majority party being Democrat, I see no problem with his quick approval. As a matter of fact, let me encourage the congress to act expeditiously."

"He certainly looks like the man I know as James F. Randall," Chase muttered under his breath, as he watched the president lead the press conference.

There was a clamor of reporters each raising their hands hoping to be recognized like a room full of first graders.

"Yes, the woman from *The Washington Post,* Ms. Sanchez."

Ms. Sanchez, a seasoned correspondent, had a reputation as a hard-hitting journalist. She rose to her feet and paused long enough for all eyes to be fixated on her. Then she read out loud her question.

"Mr. President, rumor has it that before you were sworn into office you also came under attack. Is this true?"

"Yes, Ms. Sanchez, that rumor is quite true. However, my security detail was expecting it and was able to fend off the attackers. The limousine I was in was the second one and the attackers thought I was in the first one. My driver broke away and I was never in any real danger," the president said using a controlled hand motion.

"May I ask a follow-up question?" Ms. Sanchez insisted.

"Yes, go ahead Ms. Sanchez. What is your question?" he said, with a quick nod,

"Does you administration have any idea who carried out this vicious attack against both you and President Donovan?"

"Let me say this, we have our suspicions and we are working hard on following up on them. I feel confident that we will soon learn who is behind these unprovoked and unprecedented attacks against a peace loving country and they will be brought to justice, whether they are foreign or domestic."

The cacophony resumed as hands and voices were raised to attract the President's attention. But rather than take another question, he politely thanked the press corps and turned and walked back up the red carpet, which led to the Oval Office.

The press secretary rose to his feet as the president turned to leave and stepped up to the podium. "Thank you ladies and gentlemen of the press. We have issued a written statement if you would kindly pick up one as you leave we would appreciate it. You are dismissed."

By 3:30 in the afternoon the sky had cleared and Chase returned to his office with more questions than answers. Why was the press so soft on the President? Why not ask some real questions? Who is Senator Max Wilcox really? Yes, Chase knew a little about him, who wouldn't, he was a leading senator, but why chose him? Why was Max Wilcox chosen and not the majority leader? The record showed that they were not the best of friends and at times were even political enemies, so why him? Was it political payback? Did Senator Max Wilcox know something about the new President and this was to buy his silence? Chase wrote these questions and others in his notebook for future reference.

His cell vibrated a second time. Looking at the caller ID, Chase saw it a text from Stan. The message was short and to the point ... 'We have a 911 problem.' It was Glenn and Chase's old way of communicating to each other. They had used codes and 911 meant get back to the office, it's an emergency.

# Chapter Four

"Glenn?" Stan asked, as he held the cell phone tightly against his ear. "This is Stan Berko..."

"I know who it is," Glenn interrupted. "What took you so long to call?"

Taken aback by his question, Stan heard the smile in his friend's voice. Sitting in his office on the fourteenth floor of *The New York Times,* Washington Bureau, he gaped at the phone as if it had taken on a life of its own. "How did ya know it was me? And that I would be calling?"

"It's my business to know," he said without losing a beat. "Does Chase know you called me?"

Taking a quick glance toward Chase, he nodded. "Yes, why?"

The phone fell silent before Glenn continued. "Well if this call is about what I think it is and Chase is in on it, then you guys are in deep dodo and you want me to come to the rescue. Let's talk." His voice grew intense.

Stan held up his fat hand as if to slow down his friend's eagerness. "No, my friend, let's not talk over the phone. By the way do you still fish?" he inquired.

Stan knew the answer before he asked the question. Glenn's reputation for being an avid fisherman was well established throughout the county surrounding Beaumont. Yet he asked anyway as part of the ruse he was weaving.

"Well yes, of course, why?" Glenn asked, his tone rose with interest.

"Well how about I send you a client friend of mine, and you take him to your favorite fishing hole? Let's say you two meet for breakfast tomorrow at your favorite restaurant. You guys have a nice chat, then go out and catch us some big ones," Stan said cryptically.

"Now that sounds like a terrific idea. I've been thinking I need to get out more. Send your friend on out here. I'll meet him for breakfast, my treat."

He and Glenn had become good friends since the ordeal involving The Order. It was Glenn and Chase along with Glenn's daughter Jennifer (aka Susan) who broke the plot to take over half of the United States. He owed his life to Glenn, not to mention his new and very powerful position with *The New York Times.*

"Oh say Glenn, does that lovely daughter of yours fish too?" Stan asked trying not to give anything away.

Glenn thought a minute. "Yes, yes of course, as a matter of fact, she is on a fishing trip as we speak. Don't know when she'll return."

"Well, give her our regards when you see her." Stan said, a wry smile parted his lips.

"Okay, I'll do that. Take care and I'll talk to you soon." With that they both hung up and Chase looked at Stan,

"Why the cloak and dagger? I thought you said your office was not bugged." Chase said with a raised forehead.

"It's not," looking over at a lampshade and pointing. "I was just making arrangements for a dear friend of mine to go fishing with a real pro. By the way, are you hungry?"

The sudden change of topics caught Chase by surprise, but he went along.

"Well yea, if you're buying! You want to go now? I mean don't you have to ask Mrs. Hudson's permission or something?" A grin tugging at the corners of Chase's mouth.

"Mrs. Hudson is just doing her job, she means no harm," Stan said as he wrote a quick note and gathered up some papers.

As he led Chase from his office, he took a toothpick out of the corner of his mouth and placed it precariously on the edge. The slightest movement would send it to the floor. Stan gently closed his door and locked it.

"Mrs. Hudson, I'll be out of the office for about an hour or so, but you can reach me on my cell or text me. You know the codes," he said, placing the note on her desk.

As he walked by the secretary's desk, Chase tried to think of some pithy statement to make. He decided against it, instead he just gave Mrs. Hudson a polite smile.

A moment later, they stepped out into the hall and walked to the elevator. Stan punched the button marked parking level and waited until the elevator doors opened. The dark wood paneled elevator bumped silently, and delivered them to the parking deck. Neither man spoke until they got to Stan's car.

Finally, Chase broke the silence. "So what's happened since I was in your office last?" he asked as Stan started his BMW SI.

Stan hesitated a moment and shifted his weight to one side before answering. His eyes narrowed as he described the events of the morning. "This morning, before you came into my office someone bugged my office." he confessed as if he'd committed some dark sin.

"When? How? Why?" Chase sputtered.

"Well, for starters it must have been last night," Stan said, as he pulled out on to G Street and headed east away from the White House. He turned right on Thirteenth Street and pulled in at his favorite restaurant ... the M & S Grill.

"Man I love this place," Stan said, "just smell those steaks and onions."

Chase wasn't hungry; at least he wasn't until they pulled into the parking lot just two blocks from the White House. Stan paused the conversation and led Chase into the diner.

Once inside, a wiry waitress with frazzled hair and a raspy voice greeted them. "Table or booth?"

Stan nodded in the direction of the back, and she made a quick about face. "Follow me, honey."

As they weaved past small clusters of smartly dressed men and women, Chase glanced around at the quaint café'. Its tin ceiling and brass fixtures spoke of nostalgia, of tradition, of mystique.

Taking their seat, Chase rubbed his hands over the rich mahogany table with a beveled glass top, and wondered what twist Stan had up his sleeve.

After placing his drink order, an Arnold Palmer, a mixture of half iced tea and half lemonade, Stan sat back and stared across the table.

As the waiter receded, Chase resumed his inquiry. "I thought you always left a toothpick or something on our desk in a certain position. If was in a different position when you returned that would indicate that someone had been in your office."

The etched lines in Stan's face told more than his words. "Yes, I always leave something in my office, a toothpick, a dime, a pencil, something lying in a certain way; if it is moved then I know someone has been in my office. But nothing was moved. That's what's got me baffled. I have standing orders; no one is allowed to enter my office if I am not present. I learned that from Ms. C."

A couple years earlier, Ms. Conley left Jimmy Stevens in her office with some very important documents. It cost her life and it was the undoing of The Order. Stan would never forget that lesson.

"So how did you discover that your office was bugged?" Chase fingered the menu as he spoke.

Stan's gaze shifted and he lowered his voice. "I don't know why, but I had a funny feeling that I was being watched and so I wand-ed the place. I got a reading just as I passed the lampshade on the end table."

A look of concern clouded Chase's face. "Well, why was your office bugged in the first place? You're not a criminal or some drug king pin. Are you Stan?"

Leaning in closer, Stan continued, "No, but if anybody knows anything in this town, it's me. My office is the hub of what's happening in Washington."

Chase's shoulders rose and fell. "So how much do you think whoever has been listening knows?" he probed.

Stan held his breath and let it out slowly. "They probably know what you and I know ... that the real vice president is alive and is in hiding somewhere and that you and I are on to them. That puts you and me in grave danger. If they are willing to kill the two most important men in the world, they sure as heck won't stop with them. They will come looking for us as well. Now what they plan on doing with that knowledge is a mystery to me. I just hope they don't figure out what I was talking about when I spoke to Glenn. If they do and they have evil plans, his life may be in jeopardy as well."

Chase ran his hand through his straw-colored hair. "Well why did you let me go blabbering on? You should have signaled me or something," he said as the waitress brought his meal.

"You blurted it out before I could stop you, that's why. I just hope they don't figure out the VP's code name and password."

Chase eyed Stan speculatively. "Okay, so who is this client

that you're sending to meet Glenn?" he asked between bites.

His boss stared back at him without blinking. "You ... you are the client and I want you on a plane by seven o'clock tonight."

Nearly choking on his tea, Chase sputtered, "What about Megan?" his voice etched with concern. "I can't just fly off to Colorado without as much as a good-bye. Shouldn't I call her and let her know I won't be home for dinner?"

"No," Stan said with a raised hand, "I've already taken care of it. The note I left with Mrs. H. instructed her to make arrangements with the airline and your wife. I have asked for her permission to allow me to keep you for a few days."

Chase leaned back, his eyebrows raised questioningly.

"Oh really? She's that easily bamboozled hmm?" he asked with a twisted smile.

"Yes," Stan lied. He wasn't completely honest with Megan, but he intended to clear things up just as soon as Chase was on that plane.

***

The flight to Denver departed at 8:10 p.m. and arrived at 11:44 p.m. without event. He arrived at Denver's busy airport, rented an SUV, and headed across country to the town of Beaumont. Chase pulled into the one hotel that still had its light on around 1:30 in the morning. Once he got checked in, he found his room, and crashed without undressing.

# Chapter Five

The first rays of sun sliced through the hotel's tattered curtains, and jabbed Chase in the eyes. Squinting, he threw off the blankets, stomped to the window and yanked them together, only to find shafts of light poking through the outside edges. Frustrated by the annoyance, Chase relented and marched to the bathroom and stared into the mirror. Two bleary eyes stared back. "Well, might as well get started," he muttered, and splashed a handful of cold water on his face.

Tuesday morning had come too early, yet Chase felt exhilarated. It had been years since he'd been to his adopted home of Beaumont, Colorado, as he called it, and he was excited to see the old places where he'd gotten his start. A thousand memories flooded his mind and he wished he had Megan at his side. Anxious to get started, he quickly changed into a new pair of jeans, downed a flannel shirt and laced up a new pair of hiking boots, which he'd bought in the Denver airport, and headed out to breakfast.

The Colorado air was crisp and clear as he walked the short distance from his hotel to Maxine's Diner. Chase missed eating at the old place, having spent a lot of time there during his years as a cub reporter with *The Beaumont Observer*. This was as close to home cooking as he could get, having eaten there two, sometimes three times a day. His mind went back to the first time he met Glenn Tibbits. Never in a million years would he have imagined the changes that one meeting would bring. Now he was going there to meet Glenn again.

He wondered what changes this meeting would bring.

Stepping inside, the aroma of fresh coffee mingled with bacon and eggs awoke Chases' senses. It was the peak of the breakfast hour and Maxine's Diner was packed with policemen, firemen, and utility workers. People from all walks of life made this a regular stop in the daily routine of Beaumont.

In the back sat an elderly gentlemen dressed in overalls. His snow-white hair curling out from under the fishing cap he was wearing; it was his favorite. Several other ol' timers were standing around his table laughing about something trivial. As Chase approached, the group parted, revealing a distinguished figure. It was Glenn, his face strong and lined with years of service to his country. Although the years had taken much since the last time he had seen him, yet to Chase, the older gentleman's eyes were still a crisp cool blue that seemed to pierce through Chase's soul.

"Chase, it's so good to see you again. Please sit down," Glenn said with a smile, as the two shook hands warmly.

Chase eyed the old diner with affection. "Doesn't this remind you of another meeting we once had?"

The elderly man nodded. "Yes Sir, it does. I was just

thinking back to the first time we met here as I walked over." He paused in reflection.

"I wonder what this meeting will bring," Chase said in a low tone, his eyes held Glenn's steady gaze.

Glenn nodded knowingly. "Well the changes have already begun and it may be up to us to change things back again."

They ordered breakfast and chatted about their lives.

"I wonder why Stan called you into this mess, aren't you retired?" Chase asked, as he mixed his scrambled eggs with his cheese grits.

"Well there's not a lot of people in Washington, D.C. I trust. If what I think is going on is true, then I would gladly come out of retirement."

"Do you know what Stan was talking about when he called?" Chase asked between bites.

"I have been monitoring the chatter and I have my instincts. After all, I have been in the uh ... 'information' business for a long time," Glenn said in a hushed tone.

Glenn's face gave away no secrets as the two men finished their meal in silence. It was all Chase could do to keep from asking the obvious question, but he held back, letting Glenn tell him what he needed to know in his own time.

When they finished their breakfast, Glenn laid a twenty dollar bill on the table, stood and bowed to the waitress. "Thank you, my lady, for another delightful breakfast."

She swatted him on the shoulder playfully and snatched up the twenty. "I see you're still printing your own money," she kidded.

"Yep, got the ink on the fingers to prove it." After giving her a quick hug, he led Chase outside.

Pointing to his pick-up truck, which was loaded with fishing gear, he said, "I'm parked over there. I hate getting dings in my doors because someone parked too close."

This was not news to Chase. He'd heard this excuse for parking in the only shady spot in the parking lot before. Chuckling to himself, he climbed into the cab. A few minutes later, they were rumbling out of town in the direction of Glenn's favorite fishing hole.

"How's Jennifer these days," Chase asked, trying to keep his voice level. Though he was happily married, he still remembered those long days they spent researching the backgrounds of the membership of The Community First Church.

A twinkle filled Glenn's eyes. "Oh she's fine. The agency has her out on assignment currently. I'm not at liberty to disclose her whereabouts at this time. You understand don't you?"

"I thought she had a cushy desk job," Chase interjected.

Glenn inhaled and let it out slowly. "Yeah well, the guys at the top thought they needed the best in the business. That got her out of the office and into the field after about two weeks. And they were right in doing so, if I do say so myself."

Shifting the gears, he gave chase a sideways glance. "How's Megan?"

For the next dozen miles, Chase filled him in on their life together. The more he talked, the deeper he missed her, and wished he could call her. If only he could hear her taunting voice once more before he plunged into the unknown, but alas, secrecy was the name of the game.

As they neared the fishing hole, Glenn's face grew taught. "Now that we've gotten caught up on our lives, we need to talk about today's events and what we need to do to straighten things out," he said as he took a left fork in the road. "Once we get to the river we can talk openly," he suggested.

Chase nodded. There was something in his tone that told him his life was about to take a major turn.

Precisely twenty minutes later they turned off the main road and bounced along a rutted, well-worn dirt road which lead to the river. Glenn pulled the truck into a thicket that nearly obscured its presence and got out. The two men collected their fishing gear and took a narrow path which lead down to the river and got set up with each of them handling two or three fishing poles. Chase found a large rock to sit on while Glenn stood. And so began the real reason for Chase's visit.

"So tell me about the phone call you got from the vice president, Chase. By the way, have you heard from him since your phone call?"

Chase stared at Glenn in disbelief, "Now how did you know about my phone call from the VP? Did Stan tell you about it?"

The lines around Glenn's eyes deepened. "You clearly don't know how well connected I am, do you Chase?" he said after a long pause.

Chase felt fingers of heat creeping up his neck, and he shifted uncomfortably under Glenn's benign gaze. He released a tight breath. "No. I haven't heard a word from him since the day of the assassination. They had just sworn in the vice president, or at least a man posing as the VP, as president and I got this call from a man claiming to be the real vice president. He said his caravan was ambushed and everyone was killed in an explosion from an IED. They thought they killed him too. But as chance would have it, he was never even in the vice president's limousine. A few minutes before the caravan left his residence, he decided to drive himself. The only other person who knows that he is alive is his personal bodyguard who was driving his car at the time of the attack. They are in hiding at an undisclosed location as we speak."

Glenn held his position as he digested this new information. This was a development he hadn't expected and it would require a new set of ground-rules.

"How do you know it was the vice president?" he probed as he cast out his first lure into the placid waters. The gentle ring of energy began where the lure landed and smoothly worked its way to where he stood.

"For starters, I asked him for the daily password. He knew it. It was 'cakewalk.'"

"So the vice president is alive and the man who was sworn

in as president is a fraud, and we have been given the job of uncovering who he is and what he is up to," Glenn said, as the weight of his assignment bore down upon him. He suddenly looked tired and weary beyond his years.

"Yes, and at the same time, maybe even save our nation from disaster ... again."

After a moment of introspection Glenn began to describe his activities, which lead up to their meeting. "I have been doing my own research on the people leading our government ever since the last fiasco. I just don't trust those people in Washington, D.C. You never know who they really are and what their agenda is."

Chase gave his fishing pole a quick jerk, but the fish was quicker. He reeled in his line and recast it before continuing. "Yeah, not after what happened with The Order. There were people in high places of government ready to sell out our country for the sake of political gain," he said grimly.

Glenn released a heavy sigh. "Fortunately, there were enough congressmen left to stand up for America and defend the Constitution."

"Well, how do we get enough support to impeach a sitting president when his party is in the majority and we have such flimsy evidence?" Chase asked.

Glenn lifted his rod and checked the live bait on his second pole, it was gone. "It will be extremely difficult, especially when it's the president who is leading the conspiracy?"

Shaking his head, Chase wondered out loud, "Where do

we begin with such a monumental task?"

A dragonfly lighted on the tip of Chase's pole and lingered while Glenn thought. "Well, we need to discover who he really is."

"He certainly looks and talks like the real deal. How can we prove he isn't," Chase asked, his eyebrows knit.

"DNA, or Deoxyribonucleic acid. No two people have the same DNA. There are markers in each of our DNA which identify us from each other. Forensic scientists can use DNA in blood, skin, saliva, and hair to identify a matching DNA of any individual. This process is called profiling or 'genetic fingerprinting'. The DNA profiling compares short sections of repetitive DNA between two people. It is an extremely reliable technique for identifying an individual's identity."

Time seemed to stand still as Chase considered the enormity of what his friend said. "So how do we get a sample of President Randall's DNA and compare it with the real James F. Randall's DNA?" he probed.

"As I said, I have been doing some extensive investigating on my own, I have files that you need to see on my ..."

Suddenly a shot rang out and Glenn fell forward, blood surging from a chest wound. Chase instinctively grabbed Glenn and dragged him to the safety of a large bolder as other shots rang out just missing both of them. Glenn's ashen face told Chase he was fading fast. Chase looked at his friend as he tried to stop the bleeding.

"Look Chase, we've been discovered, and your life is in

grave danger," Glenn struggled to say between bloodied coughs.

"Don't speak Glenn, save your strength," Chase said as he tore an old rag in half. He dipped it in the cool stream and began packing it into the wound.

"There's something I gotta tell ya, you gotta know." Glenn struggled to breath.

"Glenn, just hold on," Chase said as bullets ricocheted around them.

"My laptop, you gotta get my laptop, everything's—"

Glenn coughed up blood again, "everything's there—"

"Where, how, what's the password?" Chase asked franticly.

"Under the seat of the pick-up, use fishin—" he coughed again and relaxed in Chase's arms.

Suddenly, a gun slid out of Glenn's side pocket, it was a Glock 45 caliber. Chase had only used a handgun once when he went shooting with a friend back in his college days. His power of recall heightened by the sound of footsteps and the adrenaline rush he was experiencing. He checked the magazine before flicking off the safety. Then he charged the weapon and crouched lower behind the rock.

A man dressed in camouflage stepped around the corner of the bolder just enough for Chase to get a clean shot. He took aim and squeezed the trigger. The man fell back into the stream. His blood turned the crystal waters into a river of crimson. Chase crouched low, as the lifeless body began to float downstream. Still holding his position, he waited for more shooting. None came, only the babble of the water lapping over the rocks.

All at once, Chase's cell phone vibrated. He checked the caller ID and released a tense breath before answering.

"Hello."

"Chase, this is James Randall, code word, 'cakewalk.'"

Chase countered with the word, 'crosswalk'.

"Mr. Vice President are you all right? Are you in a safe and secure place?" Chase asked between gulps of air.

"Yes, how about you? Are you safe?"

"No, as a matter of fact I'm not. Are you familiar with the name Glenn Tibbits?"

"Yes, I know of him," the vice president replied rather candidly.

Chase's face tightened. "Well he and I were out here in Colorado fishing and a sniper just shot him, he died in my arms."

The phone fell silent and Chase wondered if he'd lost the connection.

"Oh my ... Are you safe? Is your life in danger?" the VP asked with growing concern in his voice.

"I was able to retrieve a hand gun out of Glenn's pocket and I got the drop on the guy. I shot him and now I've got two dead guys laying here and I don't know what to do next. I'm afraid they might come looking for me too. What should I do?" Chase paused to slow his breathing. "Glenn said he had a laptop computer in his truck with information. Should I go and get it before someone else finds it?"

There was silence on the other end of the conversation as the vice president considered his answer, "Tell you what I'd do, I'd wait unto it gets dark, and make your way back to the truck and drive to town. The sheriff of that town, what's his name?"

"Sheriff Conyers."

"Yeah, Sheriff Conyers, he can be trusted, and he will handle this very quietly. Then you get your tail outta there and back to the safety of Washington, D.C."

"Mr. Vice President, I don't think that Washington, D.C. will be much safer," Chase said as he wiped the sweat from his forehead and scanned the area.

"Just lay low until dark and get out of where you are as quietly as possible. I'll call you tomorrow at this same time and fill you in on what I know. Good-bye." The connection ended, leaving Chase to his thoughts.

Chase closed his eyes and let his ears absorb the sound around him. The minutes stretched into long hours, and he drifted to sleep

A branch snapped, and Chase jolted. What was that? His mind raced as he fingered the butt of the gun. In the darkness, a cacophony of sounds pressed in upon him and he wished he'd brought a flashlight. The moonless night closed in like an unwelcome embrace giving Chase no reprieve as he stumbled along the rugged path. He followed it until the rustle of water over rocks faded in the distance. Chase found his way back to the truck as quietly as he could, but not without stumbling several times over fallen logs and root outcroppings. With a sigh of relief, he found the truck undisturbed and the laptop under the front seat, right where Glenn indicated. He opened it up and logged on using the password Glenn had given him, and scrolled down until he found what he was looking for. Pay dirt!

# Chapter Six

C hase scanned through the files. Over the last 2 years since his retirement, Glenn built an impressive file on all of the Senators, members of the House of Representatives, the Judiciary, Cabinet appointments, and the 20 or so czars the previous President appointed. He found evidence that many of the key appointments were people who had links to The Order. Although he had exposed The Order four years earlier, it was never destroyed. It couldn't be. It was like an octopus, cut off one leg it had seven others that would wrap around you. So The Order is alive and well and back to its old tricks of infiltrating our country, Chase said to himself.

Chase returned the laptop to its place under the seat, found a flashlight and carefully checked underneath the truck for a bomb. Relieved that he found none, he pulled the key from the ashtray where Glenn left it and started the engine.

After several twists and turns, Chase found the main road leading to town and followed it. By the time he'd reached Beaumont, his wristwatch read midnight. A single street-light illuminated the empty parking lot of the old jailhouse. Suddenly, weariness washed over Chase as he stepped from Glenn's truck. Every muscle in his body screamed at him with each step, and he willed himself to the front door of the police station. Reluctantly, he grabbed the knob, turned it and stepped in.

Once inside, he was met with two bleary eyes, as Sheriff Conyers glanced up from the newspaper.

"What happened to you? You're covered in blood man!" the Sheriff said incredulously.

Chase looked down at his blood covered flannel shirt and then returned his gaze. "Hello to you too, sheriff." The two friends shook hands as Conyers motioned him to take a seat.

"Sheriff, I've got a big problem and I need your help."

"You don't say," the sheriff said as he eyed Chase wearily, "who or what did you run into? By the looks of it, it was a chainsaw."

For the next thirty minutes Chase unpacked the story of the vice president, the bug in Stan's office, and the shooting. Chase even showed the Sheriff what he found on Glenn's laptop. Conyers sat in silence taking down the pertinent information.

He seemed to deliberate for a moment before he spoke, "Son, if what you're telling me is true," he paused and looked Chase directly in the eyes, "I've got no reason to doubt you, but we got a really big problem. First let me get you a clean set of clothes. I'll send out my most discreet deputy and he will clean up the mess down at the river. In the meantime, you need to be high-tailing it out of here before you draw more attention to yourself."

Chase rubbed the back of his neck. "What about my rented

SUV and Glenn's pickup truck?"

"You and that laptop need to be in that SUV, and driving, not flying, driving back to Washington, D.C. pronto," the Sheriff said with an interesting glint in his eyes. "They may be looking for you at the airport, although I don't know why if they think the sniper did his job. But still you need to be driving."

Chase nodded and stood for a moment. "I think you're right about driving back. It might throw whoever is looking for me off the trail." He pulled out his wallet and checked his money.

"Just don't use your credit card for food or gas or anything. They might be able to track you that way. Here, here's some cash," Sheriff Conyers said, pulling a wad of bills from his uniform shirt pocket. He handed the cash to Chase, "Meantime I'll be praying for you."

Chase felt his eyebrows raise two inches. "I didn't know you were a prayin' man."

Conyers scuffed the floor sheepishly. "I haven't been until a few years ago, but the new pastor at the Community First Church is a real believer and he and I have become good friends. He took the time one day to show me from the Bible that I was a sinner, which I already knew I was. He showed me how I could have my sins forgiven." Jamming his fists into his pockets, he continued, "Chase, before I got saved, I lived a pretty sinful life. I'd done a lot of underhanded things to get and keep my job as Sheriff and I knew I needed God's forgiveness. The preacher showed me how by believing on the name of the Lord Jesus Christ, I could know for sure that when I die I'll go to Heaven. He showed me that if I committed just three sins a day, in a lifetime I would have accumulated over five hundred thousand sins. That convinced me that I needed to repent and turn to Christ. I trusted Him as my Savior and man has that made a big, big difference in my life. Heck, we even have a Bible study going on right here in this jail house."

Chase let out a big laugh and slapped him on the back, "Man that's great. Megan and I have been praying that you'd get saved. Praise the Lord!" There was a pause in the conversation, as neither knew what to say next.

"Well look, I had better be heading out of here," Chase said with a pained look on his face. "I sure feel bad about Glenn; he was one of the good guys." He let his voice trail off and his eyes misted. "I hate leaving you with this mess."

Conyers inhaled and slowly exhaled to let the tension he was feeling subside. "Don't worry about it. I'll call my pastor and we'll arrange a real nice funeral service for him and invite everyone. Glenn would have liked that. I do think though, that before this is all over, a lot of good guys and bad guys are going to fall as well. Mind if we pray?"

"Sure, I'm gonna need it," Chase said, as he bowed his head. After a short prayer the two men shook hands and parted company. Neither thought they would see each other alive again. In just a short time, Chase lost a dear friend and learned he'd gained a brother in Christ.

# Chapter Seven

S tan sat behind his massive desk and thought about his situation. I've got a bug in my office, so I can't talk freely. There is someone watching me, I can feel it, and I haven't heard from Chase in a couple of days. Megan is worried sick and I can't tell her his whereabouts. All at once, his cell phone sprang to life. He picked it up and looked at the caller ID, Chase. He checked the time. It was going on 11:00 o'clock, Tuesday morning.

"Hello Mr. Newberry, good to hear from you, it's been a while since we talked last." Stan's voice sounded unusually chipper, but Chase played along. "Why don't you and I meet for lunch as soon as you get to town, how about at the Willard?"

Chase agreed.

"Oh, and by the way, I left you a Welcome to the Family packet down at the front desk. The Welcome to the Family packet is a pack of information including a new door pass key, and badge for all new employees. When you get here, pick it up and look it over before you start your new job assignment."

Chase clearly didn't understand the melodrama, but agreed to follow Stan's instructions.

"Okay Mr. Berkowitz, I look forward to meeting with you

and getting better acquainted. How about I come by tomorrow around this time?"

"Sure, that will be fine, Mr. Newberry; see you then." He hung up the phone and rubbed his forehead as a migraine set in. *Maybe, I should drive over to Chase's house and just tell Megan what was happening so she will stop worrying and also stop calling me.*

He stood, placed a pencil on the edge of his desk and headed to his car on the parking level. He got in and turned the key. The explosion rocked the building. Flames engulfed the neighboring vehicles and Stan was gone! The automatic sprinkler system came on and by the time the fire and rescue squads arrived the flames were under control. Stan's body was burned beyond recognition.

***

The morning commute around D.C. hadn't formed a rolling parking lot yet, but it was a welcomed sight to Chase's weary eyes. It was Wednesday morning and Chase was road weary and hungry, after driving nearly straight through. Rather than stop by his house, he went directly to his office to inform Stan of the latest turn of events. When he arrived, he found yellow crime scene tape blocking off the parking level. After parking a block away Chase entered the lobby and approached the receptionist's deck on the first floor.

"What happened to the parking level?" he asked the receptionist.

She lifted her eyes and held up a finger. She quickly

finished her phone call, and said, "Oh Mr. Newton," her throat closed with emotion, "I guess you haven't heard. Mr. Berkowitz was killed yesterday by a car bomb!" She buried her face in her hands and wept uncontrollably.

Chase stood immobilized as he let the shock sink in. "A car bomb!" he repeated. "How? Why?" Chase's mind swirled like wind driven snow.

Several minutes later, the receptionist regained her composure and looked up. Her puffy eyes bore the pain Chase felt in his heart.

"That's what everyone else has been asking as well. The police have been all over this place looking for evidence and asking a lot of questions." As she spoke, her eyes darted around the lobby. Fear and pain marked their every movement.

Chase held his position, wishing he could do something, anything to relieve this woman's broken heart. She was barely hanging on emotionally.

"When did this happen?" he asked as gently as possible. "I don't know, sometime around 11:30 Tuesday morning."

*That was about the time we had talked. Apparently Stan decided to go somewhere after he talked with me.* Chase's thought fluttered like butterflies. "Is there a package for me?"

The woman sniffed back a tear and glanced around her desk. "No, nothing for you" she replied absently.

Remembering his last conversation with Stan, Chase restated his question. "Is there a Welcome to the Family packet, waiting to be picked up by a Mr. Newberry?"

The receptionist looked in the message center, "Oh yes, there is one for Mr. Newberry, would you like to have it?"

"Yes, please," Chase took it and headed to his office, hoping, just hoping for no surprises.

After greeting his secretaries and grieving over the loss of Stan, he headed to his office and closed the door. Upon opening the Welcome to the Family packet Chase emptied its contents on his desk. Rather than being new employee related stuff, it was instructions to go to a location and follow their instructions. Under no circumstances was he to tell anyone, including his wife Megan. Stan had written on a post-it stating that he was headed to Chase's house to fill Megan in on the latest events.

So that's where he was going. That means M has no clue about what's been happening. She must be worried sick.

With studied eyes Chase looked around his office wondering if it was bugged. He couldn't tell and he wouldn't trust it not to. Following Stan's instruction, Chase drove the rented SUV east on G Street to Eleventh, turned right and headed north to the intersection of Eleventh and Clifton Street. He turned left and followed it until it dead ended. The location indicated on the sheet of paper was a parking garage.

After parking his vehicle, he got out and scanned the area. The only door he could see led to a passageway. Wishing he still had Glenn's gun, he followed the passageway until it opened up to an alley. Cautiously, he started walking down a row of seedy looking shops. In nearly every doorway stood or leaned a rather unfriendly looking person. They were either guarding the door or they were functioning as a lookout; Chase couldn't tell which. As he approached one nasty looking shop, the man in the doorway stepped into his path and unceremoniously ushered him in and closed the door. After looking through the blinds he threw three or four dead bolts and flipped the Open for Business light off.

"You must be Mr. Newberry," the tattooed man said, as he looked at the paper Chase held. "You're not very good at stealth, are you?" his voice resonated in the small entry area.

Chase shifted his weight from on foot to the other. "No I guess I'm not," he said and tugged on his ear.

"Well in about an hour you better get good and stealthy," the tattooed man said sharply, "or you'll be like poor old Stan. Now stand here and let me take some pictures of you and get your measurements. While I'm creating the new you, read this." He handed Chase a dossier along with contacts and new instructions. They read like a Mission Impossible Assignment only there was no postlude saying that this document would self-destruct in ten seconds.

This was no TV show, this was a life and death struggle and he was caught in the middle of it. Two of his dearest friends had paid the ultimate price, and he could be next.

The instructions would put him in personal contact with James F. Randall, the President of the United States. Not just personal contact, but physical contact. His job was to acquire a large enough sample of his DNA that the lab boys back at the tattoo shop could analyze. Then they would compare it with another DNA sample, from the real James F. Randall. Finding, retrieving and returning with that sample would prove to be the more dangerous of the two tasks. One slip up and he would lead the enemy right to the Vice President's hiding place. How am I going to get that close to the President of the United States and make that kind of contact?

Movement caught his eyes as the man with tattoos returned carrying a full head mask, a wig, elevator shoes and some body building material. "Okay big boy, strip to the waist," he said pulling out a measuring tape.

Chase followed the man's orders, and put the mask over his head. It was like Halloween only scarier. By the time he'd finished, no one, not even he could recognized him. He was taller, stronger looking, and much darker. As a matter of fact, he was now a member of a minority and his new name was Cleve, Cleve Newberry, MD.

Along with his new name came a complete identity change including a new job. Chase, aka Cleve, was now a Medical Doctor, assigned to the President. His job was to monitor the president's physical condition on a daily basis and do a monthly physical examination. For that, Chase needed a crash course in the latest medical technology. It included CPR, how to use an AED machine, used to deliver a shock to the heart in the event that it stopped. He was also trained on how to use a Defibrillator, a machine designed for the treatment of life-threatening cardiac arrhythmias or ventricular fibrillation.

Chase was given instructions on taking someone's blood pressure, temperature, and how to draw blood. He had to learn all of these tasks and to perform them as a professional and do it quickly. His credentials were already vetted and he was expected on the job by the end of the week.

At the same time, the current MD monitoring the president was taken to the hospital with mysterious symptoms. He had cold sweats, the shakes, and a high fever, the results of a concoction administered to him by an FBI plant working within the presidential medical detail.

Chase's job would put him even closer than that operative could get. The plan also included the covert insertion of a witch's brew that would bring the president right to Cleve's medical facility before his monthly check-up. It was as close to an assassination attempt as one could get without actually killing the president.

For the next three days, Chase underwent intense medical training. By week's end, Mr. Tattoo, as Chase called him, stepped into the room where Chase sat, crossed his arms across his sizable chest and asked, "Well Cleve, what do ya think?" A big grin stretched across his face.

"I feel like a new man," Chase said as he viewed himself in a mirror.

Mr. Tattoo nodded. "Good, you need to be, because they are expecting you tomorrow morning at 7 a.m. sharp. Have your badge on and your medical kit in hand. Wear this stethoscope at all times, and I mean ALL times. In it is a TV monitor and listening device. Also you will be wearing an ear piece which looks like a Cochlear implant, but it's not. It's a mini microphone; we can speak to you any time we need to and if you get into trouble, we have a medical team at the ready to talk you through most any crisis. You will also be monitored at all times by satellite and infrared heat sensors. You will never be out of our sight. Just don't lose those two items; if you do you're on your own. Is that clear?" Mr. Tattoo's voice sounded like a drill sergeant, and Chase felt his blood pressure hike.

"Yes Sir! Sir" he said. All he lacked was a 'Hooah.'

"Oh, by the way," the tattooed man held Chase's gaze, "your wife is fine. Ever since you left to go fishing, Megan's cousin from Wisconsin has been visiting her and will see to it that she is cared for. So don't worry about her at all, just focus on the task at hand."

Chase shook his head slowly, "What are you talking about? She doesn't have a cousin from Wisconsin."

"She does now and they will get along just fine," he said, with a toothy smile.

Pacified but not satisfied, Chase continued probing, "But why was I chosen for this job anyway, I'm not an FBI agent?"

"You are the only person that James Randall trusts and calls, so you are the go-to-guy," he said with a smile, "so let's go save the country."

# Chapter Eight

The pounding on her front door rattled Megan's nerves and she wondered who it could be. Pushing out a frustrated breath, she glanced at her watch. It was way too early for Chase to be home. Maybe he got off early; in that case we could go out for dinner and a movie, she thought.

The banging continued.

Ever since her and Chase's ordeal in Beaumont involving her parents and the sinister group calling itself, The Order, she'd become wealthy overnight; windfall from her father's overseas investments left in her name. Shortly thereafter, she'd become Mrs. Megan Newton following a simple wedding, and moved into an upper class community in the Tyson's Corner, near Washington, D.C.

With her husband's new position, came increased demands on his schedule. To help relieve some of the pressure he was under, Megan volunteered to do some research for him.

Today, she'd worked all morning and into the afternoon on a special editorial Chase asked her to research and the words weren't coming. Between several irritating phone calls and the neighbor's crying baby, she'd accomplished little. Megan pinched her lips together and laid her laptop aside hoping to deal quickly with yet another interruption and get back to her work.

She swung the door open and was immediately swallowed in an enthusiastic bear hug.

"Megan, so good to see you, I'm Linda Edwards, your cousin from Wisconsin. I'm so excited to finally meet you," she said, pushing further inside the foyer, and dropping her suitcases.

Megan stood, mouth gaped open. "But I don't have a cousin from Wisconsin."

"Oh yes you do, I found you on the internet. I just did a people search and there you were, my long lost cousin. I flew all the way from Milwaukee just to get reacquainted," she said with a big grin. "So don't just stand there, Silly, close the door and let's get caught up, it's been years and we have a lot to talk about."

With her mind swirling, Megan obeyed and closed the door. She turned to face her visitor and saw the barrel of a gun pointed between the eyes.

"Okay, now Megan, let's take this nice and easy. Come into the kitchen and let's sit and talk."

Megan's legs turned to water as she moved from the entry to the kitchen, her heart pounding like a piston.

Pointing with the gun, Linda directed Megan to the armed captain's chairs and began to wrap duct-tape around her arms.

"What is going on? Who are you and what do you want?" Megan insisted as her frozen mind began to thaw out.

Without speaking, the woman reached into her purse and took out a small elongated box. Megan's eyes widened as the woman lifted the lid and picked up a needle filled with a yellow fluid. She struggled to free herself, but the duct-tape bit into her flesh.

"Now Megan, don't make this any harder than it has to be." Then she pointed up, flicked it with her finger and inserted it into Megan's left arm.

Warmth radiated up her arm into her chest. The euphoric effect of the drug made Megan's mind swirl, then everything went black.

Quickly, the woman calling herself Linda, removed the tape from Megan's arms, threw her over her shoulder and loaded her into the trunk of her car. Then she opened the garage door, backed into the street and drove away. As she did so, she passed a parked car with a woman slumped behind the wheel. The small hole left from the 22-caliber bullet was barely visible except for the trickle of blood which ran down the side of her temple.

As the effects of the drug wore off, Megan's mind wobbled back to consciousness. The room where she sat handcuffed to an old metal chair was cold and dark. Something stiff and hard stretched across her mouth, making it hard to breath. Disoriented and nauseous from the drug, she tried to get her bearings. Outside, voices rose and fell in languages she was not familiar with.

A metal chair scraped against the concrete floor, followed

by heavy footfalls. With an eerie creek, the door opened filling the small room where she'd been sitting with a golden light. Blinking, Megan's breath caught in her throat as the form of a large woman approached.

"Well sleepy head, you finally decided to wake up?" A woman, wearing a militia uniform, said with a sneer.

Megan narrowed her eyes.

Lowering her face to Megan's, she spoke in an icy tone. "You will tell us where your husband is or you will die, it's that simple."

The command struck Megan like a bolt of lightning. Chase left for work earlier in the day and hadn't returned. The woman tore the duct tape from her mouth and Megan winched. "You tell me where your husband is and I'll not shoot you," she said and pulled a 45 caliber Rugar from behind her back.

Megan felt the color drain from her face. "I don't know what you're talking about."

The woman charged her weapon and fired in the air. Dust and chunks of ceiling material covered the two women and Megan's ears rang. A rush of adrenalin shot through her body making her hands turn to ice. She began to shake uncontrollably.

"Please you must believe me. I don't know where he is," she pleaded.

Then the woman pointed the gun at her head.

Megan closed her eyes expecting to meet her Lord at any moment. With a deafening sound, the weapon exploded and

Megan's eyes popped open. The woman stood, barrel raised inches above her head. The smell of singed hair and gun powder assaulted Megan's nose, making her eyes water. Her ears rang making it nearly impossible to hear. For an instant, her mind froze. Her muscles began to shake violently, and she gulped down the bile which crept up her throat.

Out of the corner of her eye, a well-dressed man stepped into the room. "What are you doing?" His thick Russian accent brought a sudden chill to Megan's rattled mind. "Are you trying to kill our guest? Put that weapon away and let's be hospitable."

Then he reached down and unlocked the handcuffs. The scent of his cologne made Megan wonder if she'd not met him before, but where?

"Here drink this," he said, handing her a bottle of water. The familiar ring of his voice made Megan's heart quicken. Beads of sweat formed on her forehead. I know that voice.

He turned a cold stare to the woman holding the gun and dismissed her curtly.

Returning his attention to Megan, he continued, "Young lady, please forgive my subordinate. She has no class. She's just a peasant with a gun." Then he flipped the light switch. Megan's pupils dilated in the bright light, she blinked. The Dean stood before her, glaring. She never knew his real name. All she'd ever heard him referred to was the nebulous title called, 'The Dean.' It was he one who trained her father and recommended him for the pastorate of the community First

Church in Beaumont, Colorado.

Many years earlier, The Dean stepped on the stage of time. Then, he was the Dean of Religious Studies at Bruton College in Virginia. His primary focus was on Eastern Religions with an emphasis on yoga, spirit guides and eastern mysticism. His mission was to recruit bright young people with leadership skills and bring them into the shadowy organization called The Order. His success rate was renowned. Before he came to Bruton, he had been in other institutions of high-learning. Over the past decades his influence had reached as far as Oxford in England and Cambridge in Europe. He plied his trade at Cardiff University in Wales, Chalmers in Sweden, Hasselt University in Belgium, Johannes Kepler University of Linz, Austria, Cairo University in Alexandria, Egypt, and Hellenic Open University in Athens, Greece. All of the great leaders of The Order had been, at one time, under his tutelage, and he held sway over their young impressionable minds, so it was with one of his latest students, Pastor T. J. Richards.

Megan's pulse quickened as the memories of her evil father chaffed at her mind. This man is evil incarnate.

The Dean extended his hand and led Megan out of her cell into a brightly lit room. She glanced around and saw a small group of soldiers staring back at her.

"Please sit here where it is more comfortable. Can I get you something, food, another bottle of water?" he said, his tone softening.

Megan narrowed her eyes, "Thanks, but no thanks."

Shaking his head, the man continued, "I have watched you for years and now look at you. You have grown up to be a fine young lady and a married one at that," he said with a whimsical smile. "Your father would be so proud of you. On second thought; he might be disappointed with your choice of men to marry. Speaking of that, I'm sure you must miss your husband very much. I understand he had made a real name for himself ever since that unfortunate situation with the Document and such. The sooner you help us find your husband the sooner you two can be together again."

Megan's throat constricted. *What is he talking about?* Her eyes burned with anger, with fear, and doubt.

"But enough with reminiscing," he mused. Then his grey eyes grew suddenly cold. "We need some information which only you have. It would help us tremendously if you could provide us with it." His voice was soft and tender, but Megan could see in the line of his face that he was a man of steel.

Megan blinked away his gaze and forced a faint smile.

"What kind of information?" Megan asked knowing it would be used against her husband and maybe her country.

The Dean's eyes deepened. "We do need to get in touch with your husband most urgently. Could you call him on your cell phone and allow us to speak with him? I'm sure we could come to an amicable solution to this peccadillo." A wicked chuckle percolated from his chest.

He handed her cell phone to her. With trembling fingers, she reluctantly speed dialed Chase's number.

The prerecorded message said: "The customer you are attempting to reach is out of range, please try again later."

# Chapter Nine

As expected, Dr. Cleve Newberry stepped from the limousine at exactly 7:00 a.m. Monday morning and strode confidently to the guardhouse located outside the White House. Sergeant Bruce met him with a crisp salute, which he returned in like manner. Chase had spent the previous hours of the night reading his Bible and praying for Megan, himself, and the mission until God gave the assurance he sought.

"Good morning Dr. Newberry, you have been expected. We have a vehicle waiting for you, please step this way. If you will follow Sergeant Hudson, he will escort you to the medical facility where you are assigned."

Dr. Newberry turned to the sergeant and followed him to a waiting golf cart. The ride was not long and the warm sun filtered through the trees as they meandered to the back of the White House. It reminded Chase of former days when he and his dad would spend a day on the golf course.

Chase couldn't help but notice the immaculately manicured lawn and shrubbery as he passed through the White House grounds. As they approached the rear entrance, two Marines stood guard. Following their sharp salute, Sergeant Hudson led the doctor into the lower level of the stately building.

"Just follow me and I'll get you squared away in your office," the sergeant said.

With a stiff gait, he led him down one corridor, which led to another corridor, which opened up to a row of doors. The third door on the right marked Medical Examiner was where they were headed. His gloved hand grabbed the door knob and swung the door open. "After you, Sir," he said, and allowed Dr. Newberry to step inside. "This is Nurse Hodges. She will assist you from here. Have a wonderful day, Sir." He turned crisply and walked back down the corridor.

Chase stood for a moment and watched the woman dressed in a nurse's uniform rise and approach him.

"Good morning Dr. Newberry," Nurse Hodges said in a friendly tone. She stood, walked around her desk and glanced at his badge. Then she extended her hand. "On behalf of the president, his family, and the White House staff, welcome."

A warm smile tugged at the corners of her mouth. Suddenly, a wave of recognition swept over Chase and his breath caught in his throat. For a moment, Chase stood trying to place her voice. Quickly regaining his thoughts, he returned her smile. A voice in his earpiece made a wisecrack.

I heard nothing about serving the first family and all the White House staff in this gig, His mind sputtered.

"Thank you for this warm welcome, I trust my services will be needed as little as possible."

"That's the best you can come up with?" a voice said in

his ear piece. Chase cleared his throat.

Nurse Hodges shook her head in a womanly fashion.

"Oh, on the contrary, your services will be quite in demand. There is always someone coming down with something, or getting hurt somehow. This is one of the busiest places in the White House," she said as she brushed a strand of hair out of her eyes.

Chase hesitated to answer too quickly, then scanned the room, "Where is my examination room? I'd like to get acclimated with everything."

Nurse Hodges moved with the finesse of a ballroom dancer as she led him into the adjoining room. It was set up pretty much the way his training room had been.

Chase put his hands on his hips and let out a slow whistle, "Good, this looks well-lit and well equipped. I don't think that I'll need to requisition any new equipment," he said as he looked around.

Nurse Hodges nodded. "If you do need anything, let me know and I'll start the paperwork. We just might get it before the end of the president's term of office. Literally, it takes an act of congress to get something new around here."

The door in the outer office slammed and Mr. Edwards, the Chief of Staff, walked into the examination room. His lips tightly stretched across a set of pearly white teeth as he spoke. "Nurse, why aren't you manning the reception desk? And why are you back here with the Dr.? I'm sure Dr. Newberry has his hands full without you bothering him. Go back to work and let me handle the good doctor?"

Mr. Edwards was a scheming little man with an attitude. Chase saw he was good at making enemies very quickly. His angular face and squinty eyes only accentuated his harsh personality. The intel he was given was indeed accurate.

He squared himself directly in front of Chase and snapped, "Dr. Newberry, I don't know how you pulled it off, but you're here now and as much as I don't like it, you and I are on the same team. But understand one thing; you will do nothing without *my* permission. I control access to the president! I control his schedule, and I will get you fired if I see you step out of line. Do you understand me?"

"Yep! Right on cue. Looks like Mr. Chief of Staff is the same as he's always been," said a voice in Chase's earpiece. Cleve, scratched the back of his neck and replied respectfully,

"Oh Yes, Sur! Sur, is there anything else massah?" Chase said in his best Afro-American English.

The Chief of Staff's eyes widened. With a huff, he turned on his heels and stomped toward the door. "Pack up your gear and be at the back entrance. We leave in five minutes," he said over his shoulder. A moment later, he was gone.

"Chase poked his head from the doorway and offered Nurse Hodges a mischievous grin. "How'd I do?"

Nurse Hodges smiled back. "You did good for your first day on the job. Now let's get a move on, grab your medical bag and follow me."

She was nearly in a run as she left the White House

Medical Facility with Dr. Newberry close on her heels.

"Where are we going?" he said between gasps.

"To the helo pad. It looks like the president is going somewhere, and wherever he goes, we go," she said as she reached the exit.

Outside the service entrance, a black Lincoln with flags on the front fenders awaited. Sergeant Hudson stood by the vehicle ready to close the door as soon as they got in. Dr. Newberry followed his nurse and slid into the car. The door closed behind them with a soft thud and they looked at each other.

"All set?" The driver asked. Without waiting for an answer, he gunned the engine. Chase and Ms. Hodges were thrown backwards into the plush seats as the Lincoln sped toward the helicopter landing pad. Within a few minutes they were sitting next to a large helicopter. The presidential entourage, including Chase and his medical team of one, loaded into it. A minute later, lifted off sending grass clippings and dust into the cool morning air.

"Navy One to Air Force One: our ETA is ten minutes, do you copy?" asked the pilot of the helicopter mechanically.

"Copy that Navy One, see you in ten, over and out," said the voice from Air Force One.

Exactly ten minutes later, the helicopter touched down yards away from a massive airplane with Air Force One painted on the tail fin. The president, followed by his personal staff, disembarked the helicopter and made their way up the stairway to the plane followed by the press corps.

Chase stepped into the fuselage of Air Force One and took a seat. He could hear the muttered complaints of his former colleagues as they found their way in. Complaints he'd made. Now, sitting in the area designated for the medical team, he bit back a grin, thankful for the comfortable seat.

After becoming airborne, the captain turned off the seat belt light and announced that they were allowed to move about the cabin.

"Dr. Newberry," Nurse Hodges whispered.

It took a moment for Chase to realize she was speaking to him.

"Dr. Newberry, would you follow me? I will take you to the medical clinic."

He gave her a questioning look and followed her.

The medical clinic, located one floor down from the main flight deck, was a complete medical clinic. Everything he needed was at his fingertips. He just hoped his services weren't needed.

"Do you know where we are going?" Chase asked as he scanned the room.

Nurse Hodges nodded. "Yes, they briefed us yesterday. We are headed to Somalia. The president will be attending a conference on global warming. He was invited by the Somalian government to join them in a signing ceremony. The two nations are some of the last countries not to have signed the UNFCCC. They plan on signing it as a joint venture. He'll be making a speech and is expected to sign The Kyoto Protocol treaty as well. If you ask me, that treaty will just about destroy our economy and intrude upon our sovereignty as a nation. I wish he wouldn't sign it."

"Sorry about that chief," Chase heard in his earpiece. "Great, I wish I knew about this before today, I would have brought my suntan lotion." a wry smile tugged at the corners of his lips.

Nurse Hodges shrugged her shoulders nonchalantly, "Don't worry Dr.," she reached out and squeezed his hand. "We won't be out in the sun too much."

Chase nodded, stepped behind his desk and sat down. *What is it about Nurse Hodges that reminds me of somebody else? Was it the way she spoke? Or the way she squeezed my hand?* He pondered a moment.

Unannounced, Mr. Edwards barged into his office and interrupted his thoughts. "Dr. Newberry, the president has asked to see you in the Presidential Suite, immediately. Drop what you are doing and follow me."

He did a sharp about face and marched out with Chase close behind. "Now listen carefully to my instructions. You'll say 'Yes Mr. President, No Mr. President' none of this Afro-America jargon, do you understand me?"

Chase bit back a smile with a somber. "Yes Sur!"

Edwards' eyes narrowed to an icy stare. He spun on his heels and led Chase down the narrow passage. The two men arrived at the door or the Presidential Suite a moment later. It was flanked by two large Marines in dress uniform. The Chief of Staff knocked lightly and a voice from within said, "Enter."

The Chief of Staff opened the door and stepped in followed by Chase.

"Sir, this is Dr. Cleve Newberry your Chief Medical Examiner."

"Thank you, Mr. Edwards that will be all." The president reached out his hand and shook Chase's.

"Dr. Newberry, it's a pleasure to meet you, please take a seat. You never know when this plane might hit an air pocket and you go up and hit your head on the ceiling of the plane," said the President as he assessed the doctor.

Nervously, Chase took his seat and glanced around the miniature version of the Oval Office. On the carpeted floor was the Presidential seal, and the United States flag stood behind the desk. Chase's trained eyes began studying the president's mannerisms as he began to relax in his cushioned seat. He interviewed Randall on numerous occasions and noticed several idiosyncrasies about him. The man he knew as the vice president had a habit of touching his fingers to the top of the desk as he spoke. It was a small movement often used to emphasize an important point, but one he repeated. Chase watched the president as he spoke, not once did he touch the top of the desk. Chase made a mental note of the subtle change.

The president's next statement captured his attention again. "Dr. Newberry, I noticed in your records that you are a

Navy man. You served on the USS Theodore Roosevelt and saw a bit of action during Operation Desert Storm in 1991," the president's piercing blue eyes seemed to penetrate Chases' outer shell.

Chase nodded slightly. "Yes Sir, I was a much younger man back then." Remembering to use his best grammar.

The president's expression didn't change as he continued. "That was before David Architzel assumed command of the USS Theodore Roosevelt wasn't it?"

"Yes Sir, I served under David J. Venlet," he said having memorized his dossier thoroughly.

The president opened a folder and glanced down at a few scribbled notes. "I also see here that you were awarded the Navy and Marine Corps Medal for sea rescues, involving risking your life."

Chase released a tight breath and smiled. "Yes, Sir, and I would do it again if I had to."

The president considered his last statement for a moment. "Well Dr. Newberry, it is good to have you on board my team. I am told that I am scheduled to come to your office next week for a check-up."

Chase hesitated not wanting to sound too eager. "Yes Sir and I look forward to giving you a clean bill of health."

After having concluded his brief interview, the president smiled and rose to his feet. Again he extended his hand and the two men shook hands firmly.

"Thank you Dr., that will be all for this time. Have a nice

flight. Oh, and be sure to stop by the Executive Dining Room and order the biggest steak we have on-board. Tell them it's on the house, compliments of the President."

Mr. Edwards, the Chief of Staff, stepped back in the Presidential suite and ushered Chase out.

"That will be all Doctor. They need you back in the clinic, so you had better get a move on," he snapped.

Chase reentered the Medical Clinic and found a Secret Service agent bleeding from the nose.

"What happened to you, did you get into a fight with a door jamb?" The agent nodded.

"Yes, Sir, that last air pocket we hit sent me right into the bulkhead and wham-o, to the moon," he said as he lightly touched the purple wound on his nose and upper lip.

"Relax Chase, this is routine stuff," said the voice in his earpiece. "Just apply pressure on the pressure point under his jaw, and put a roll of gauze up under his front lip. Tell him to hold his head back and that should stop the bleeding."

Chase followed the instructions and to his surprise it worked. His first patient survived. Chase felt great.

For the next sixteen hours Chase shifted between administering bandages and dispensing pills. After his last patient, a reporter suffering from a stomach virus, was dismissed, the pilot's voice came over the intercom instructing everyone to prepare for landing.

The giant plane landed in Mogadishu, the capitol, and taxied to a halt near a small building, which served as the

Airport Terminal. A set of stairs was rolled out to the side of the plane with a large red carpet at its base. A military detail, led by a heavily decorated four star general marched briskly forward and took their positions on either side of the carpet. The general's patent leather shoes tapped lightly on the metal steps. With a crisp movement he saluted the president and guided him down.

At the bottom, the presidential limousine and several more Lincoln Town cars waited. The presidential detail loaded their respective vehicles and departed, headed for the Presidential Palace.

The lead car was filled with Secret Service personnel, the second car was a decoy, and the third car held President Randall, and Dr. Newberry was assigned to the fifth car back. Following them was another vehicle with Secret Service personnel and then the press corps.

As Chase stepped from the shadow of the massive aircraft, he was greeted by a blast of acrid, dry air. The temperature must have been 110 degrees in the shade. His first breathe nearly seared his lungs and he wondered how anyone could exist in such an extreme environment. He placed a new pair of Izod Polaroid sunglasses on his face and hoped the heat wouldn't deteriorate his disguise. Fortunately he was only exposed to the brutal heat for the few moments it took to descend the stairs and enter the waiting Lincoln Town car. By then, he was sweating profusely as was his nurse. He settled into his seat and buckled the seat belt and looked around at the stark scenery.

"This sure is a lot hotter than I ever imagined; maybe next time we can land somewhere in Antarctica," Chase said as he mopped his brow with a handkerchief.

Nurse Hodges smiled and brushed the hair behind her ear. A look of concern filled her face. She was clearly uncomfortable with her current circumstance. The motorcade pulled out and left the confines of the airport. It wormed its way along the pot-hole ridden highway until it neared a population center. The houses and people closed in and Chase suddenly felt claustrophobic.

Somalia has a history of violence. Ever since the Civil War in 1991 when Ethiopian backed forces ousted President Barre, the country had been in upheaval. In 1993, Mohamed Farrah Aidid was responsible for leading an attack against an American helicopter resulting in nineteen American soldiers and a thousand of his countrymen being killed.

# Chapter Ten

Without warning, the streets of Mogadishu jolted to life as the lead vehicle jolted upright as a large bomb exploded underneath it. The car flew into the air and landed upside down on the second car. Immediately, the air was filled with gunfire as the ambush ensued. It was as if someone had kicked a beehive the way the bullets swarmed around each of the stalled vehicles.

The president's car came under fire as the insurgents took aim on it. Quickly, the other vehicle with Secret Service agents pulled along-side of the president's car and gave it cover on the right side. The car Chase was in pulled alongside on the left. They had come to a standstill for the moment as the head of security assessed the situation.

"Incoming," screamed the Chief of Staff as a rifle propelled grenade struck just in front of the presidential vehicle. The explosion tore through the windshield killing the driver instantly. The president exited the burning vehicle and took cover between cars. In the face of a withering barrage of bullets, Chase jumped from the relative safety of his vehicle and grabbed the president by the arm and dragged him back into his car.

"Mr. President, are you okay?" Chase asked as he noticed

him hold his side. The answer was obvious. Blood was seeping through the president's shirt. Nurse Hodges grabbed his medical kit and began pulling packing material from it and handed it to Chase.

"Pack the wounds, we gotta stop the bleeding," said the voice in his earpiece. Chase acted quickly with what little trauma training he had.

Chase took the president's face in his hands and spoke directly to him, "Mr. President, can you breathe all right?"

"Yes, but I think a piece of shrapnel pierced my bullet proof vest."

Chase ripped open the president's shirt only to find a bulletproof vest protecting the man's upper body. He released the Velcro which held it in place and removed it just long enough to find the wound.

Sweat beaded on Chase's upper lip as he realized the gravity of the situation. The man he was sent to expose as an impostor lay wounded next to him and it was his responsibility to save the man's life. Chase fished his finger in the wound. "There it is. We gotta get that thing out without it doing any more damage."

The area of the wound was on the lower left of the abdomen, and to the best of his knowledge there were no vital organs in the immediate area. Chase felt around the area of the entry wound, took a calculated guess, and found the end of the shrapnel. The bulletproof vest blunted most of the impact, but the piece of metal had punctured the abdominal wall and produced a lot of bleeding. With care, Chase removed the piece and packed the wound with gauze.

Outside of the car, the battle continued on with no sign of abating. Several secret service agents had been wounded and were lying where they fell. With the president's condition under control, Nurse Hodges jumped from the car and was attending to one of the fallen men. Chase knew that if they didn't get out of this situation fast, all would be lost. He made a radical decision. The driver of his vehicle had exited the car and was returning fire. Chase jumped over the front seat and slammed it in reverse and sped backwards. Just then another RPG hit the ground near by leaving a gaping hole. He did a 180 degree turn and headed back to the safety of the airport and prayed that Air Force One was not doing the usual practice touch-and-go exercises. Fortunately for Chase, the plane hadn't moved. He made a beeline to the stairway and screeched to a halt. The security detail protecting Air Force One had already taken up positions when the head of the security detail called in the attack.

"Mr. President," Chase said, gulping air, "can you make it out of the car?" without waiting, he jumped out and came around to the side of the car where President Randall sat, holding his side.

A pained expression registered on his face. "Yes, but I'll need some help up those steps."

Chase put the president's right arm over his shoulder and guided him up the stairs while other staff members came along side to help them. Once Chase got the president squared away, he turned to leave.

The president looked up from the gurney he was lying on. "Where are you going, Son?" he asked, his face marked with concern.

Chase paused at the bulk-head and turned. "Look, Mr. President," the lines in his eyes etched in worry, "I left my nurse on the ground helping the wounded and I'm not leaving her."

President Randall nodded thoughtfully. "Doc, this plane is leaving immediately and if you're not on it you'll be left behind."

"Well, so be it, I'm not going to let an unarmed white lady fall into the hands of that angry mob." Turning, he stepped off the plane.

In his earpiece Chase could hear Mr. Tattoo saying, "the mission, don't forget the mission."

"Forget the mission, I'm not leaving Ms. Hodges to a pack of angry wolves," he said as he descended the stairs and climbed back into the shot-up Lincoln Town car. He slammed the door shut, put the car in gear and sped back into harm's way.

The battle continued, but seemed to have slacked somewhat. Chase pulled up to the encircled cars and jumped out and grabbed one of the wounded men. Nurse Hodges grabbed another and dragged him to the car. One of the remaining secret service agents followed suit by taking the

Chief of Staff by the arms and literally tossing him into the waiting vehicle. The remaining detail all piled in as Chase jammed the car back in reverse and repeated the trip.

At some point in time Chase realized that someone was screaming in his ear piece. His back-up team had been trying to get his attention, but with all of the explosions and gunfire it was hard to hear. By the time Chase could give it any attention, most of the danger was behind him. He chose to ignore whoever was screaming at him. As he approached the airport he saw Air force One lifting its nose skyward. Chase's heart sunk like a rock. *Oh no! We're stranded in a foreign country full of angry, America-hating people and no way out!*

"Look Doctor," said one of the agents, "there's a C17 getting ready to take off. It's one of our support planes and it may be our only hope of getting out of here."

The rear ramp was still down as if it were the jaw of a hungry alligator.

"If I can catch up to that plane maybe I can drive this car right up the ramp before it lifts off," Chase announced with a look of determination in his eyes.

An agent leaned over the front seat. "It's risky, but what's our chance if we hang around this dump," he said as he watched a caravan of jeeps and SUV's loaded with gun toting Somalians giving chase.

Chase spun the car around and headed in the direction of the C17. Watching the speedometer inch past 80, then 90 miles an hour, Chase gripped the steering wheel tighter and held his breath. The car lurched forward as it accelerated to 100 miles. As he positioned the vehicle directly behind the speeding C17, he had to work to hold it steady as it passed through the jet wash. With the ramp still down, sparks flew up and hit his windshield as it scraped along the tarmac. Chase nosed the car directly behind the mammoth airplane and gunned the engine. It lunged forward, hit the edge of the ramp, and bounced. As the rear wheels caught hold, it suddenly raced up the ramp. Were it not for the cargo netting, the car would have driven out of control right into the flight deck. The netting held and the car slammed to a halt. A moment later, the bay door closed and the mighty plane rose into the air. A cheer went up from the flight crew but went unnoticed by Chase and those in the car.

"Man that was close; everybody Okay?" Chase asked, looking around the passenger compartment.

"Sir, we've got two wounded, one KIA, and three able-bodied people on board, Nurse Hodges said."

A lump formed in Chase's throat, and he swallowed hard. "Who was killed?"

Moments stretched and Nurse Hodges let out a tight breath. "It's Mr. Edwards, the Chief of Staff," she whispered.

Their eyes met as each read the other's thoughts. "That's too bad, I didn't even have a chance to tell him about the Lord," Chase said with true sorrow in his heart.

A moment of silence passed. "The rest of you are okay?" Chase asked, looking at his nurse for confirmation.

"A bit shaken up, but we'll make it. Thanks for coming

back and to get us. If you didn't, we'd all be dead by now," said one agent as he patted him on the shoulder.

"Yes Sir, Doc. All but one of us were out of ammo. If you hadn't returned when you did, we wouldn't have made it. We all owe you our lives. Thank you," said another one of the security detail.

Static crackled in Chase's earpiece, as cheers echoed from his support team.

# Chapter Eleven

Vice President Randall tried his cell phone again only to get the same results – 'the party you are attempting to reach is out of range.'

For the first time James Randall began to worry. The only man who could prove his identity could very well be dead.

He and his only body guard found a safe place to hide, but it would only be a matter of time before someone discovered his whereabouts and called the people who sought his life. He had to keep moving, but the more he moved the greater the chance they would pick up his trail. There was only one place to hide where they would not think of looking, but getting there was a problem. Keeping it a secret was even a bigger problem.

*How had this happened?* The vice president kept asking himself. *How could this have taken place? The best informed, best protected, best insulated men in the world were ambushed simultaneously. This could only have happened with a lot of insider information. It is obvious there are moles in our administration. But they all couldn't be traitors; surely someone loyal to the president would have stepped forward and let the chief of security know about a plot to assassinate the president and vice president. Maybe that explains why several of the members of my security detail suddenly turned up missing last week.*

He let his mind wander back to the days early in the presidency. President Donovan had won a landslide victory over the liberal democrat challenger and his coattails swept in a majority of his colleagues. It looked like they had a mandate to implement many of the sweeping reforms that he (they) had promised on the campaign trail. All that changed in a moment. Everything they'd worked for now hung by a thread and even that was showing signs of strain.

In the short time he had been in office the new president, the most liberal of his party, had taken steps to liberalize trade agreements with countries that were known for harboring terrorists and were guilty of human rights violations. While at the same time he snubbed those countries who had been our friends and allies down through the years.

If the signing of the Kyoto Treaty is enacted Vice President Randall knew he had an uphill climb to turn things around if he ever got back into office. The stakes were high and the risks were even higher.

\*\*\*

Megan knew she couldn't have been taken far, and guessed, by the volume of traffic outside, she was still in Washington, D.C. the room which held her captive was unheated and she shivered as the temperature outside dropped. The thin garment she'd been wearing when she was abducted did little to keep out the chill. The icy grip of the handcuffed and the cold metal chair added to her discomfort. Her cell phone lay on the table next to her, mockingly. All she had to do was call her husband and her captors would do the rest, but she couldn't do it. It wasn't that she hadn't tried. Nothing would bring her more comfort than to hear her husband's voice, yet every time she called, she got the same message – 'the party you are trying to reach is out of range.'

*After all that we have been through, did it all have to come down to this?* Megan let her mind drift back to the time when they first met ... more than three years ago. Her first recollection of seeing Chase was when she barged into his dusty office in *The Beaumont Observer* and asked him if he would help her learn the journalism business. She was the editor of her junior college's newspaper and he was a cub reporter. He was the kind of guy who thought he knew it all, and he had a reputation for demonstrating it. She obviously didn't make a big impression on him the first time they met. Either that or maybe he already had a girlfriend; she couldn't tell. But Megan was used to getting her way. The second time she saw him, she tried to make a bigger impression. Her attempt at running him over in the crosswalk definitely got his attention. She smiled at the thought as she sat handcuffed to the chair. He claims it was that silly impulsive act that got the whole series of events started. It ended in her becoming a multi-millionaire and the wife of Mr. Chase Newton.

*How could these people be the same evil people that she and Chase exposed?* She thought. *I thought that The Order was defeated. Why was this evil man who called himself 'The Dean' involved in abducting me? And why do they want my husband?*

The only thing she could think of was … they wanted revenge.

Megan prayed.

# Chapter Twelve

Sheriff Conyers made all the arrangements for Glenn's funeral. He called his pastor, and asked him to lead a funeral with an emphasis on worship and celebration. Since Pastor T.J.'s disappearance the church was left with only a few remaining members and an open pulpit. The pulpit committee moved quickly to fill the vacancy. This time, they spent much more time praying rather than reading resumes. God led a very godly young man to the church and he proved to be just what the hurting, beleaguered church needed.

Pastor Steve Callahan graduated from a fundamental Bible college in the mid-west and was anxious to establish a strong witness for Christ in that part of Colorado. He was prayerful and fervent, a real man of the Word. His zeal brought him to Sheriff Conyers' jail where he led several detainees to the Lord. That's how the Sheriff heard the gospel as well. His conversion affected the whole way he ran the police department. No more informants, no more under the table deals. From now on Sheriff Conyers was an honest broker. The change that Christ made in his life was immeasurable and the whole community took notice of it. So when the death of Glenn Tibbits was announced from the pulpit of the Community First Church, many people called for Sheriff

Conyers to take the lead in making the funeral arrangements.

Once again the church was packed out as friends and well-wishers came from miles around to give their last respects to a man who embodied godliness.

Pastor Callahan opened the service with a simple prayer followed by a brief eulogy. Rather than having a soloist sing, Sheriff asked the organist to play an old favorite and the congregation sang along. Pastor Callahan read from John 11:25, "Jesus said unto her, I am the resurrection, and the life: he that believes in me though he was dead, yet he shall live."

Then he turned his attention to the grieving assembly and spoke encouragingly. "Friends of Glenn Tibbits, we are here to celebrate the home-going of a dear saint of God. The bodily form of Glenn remains, but he is alive and well in Heaven with Christ his Savior. That happened the moment Glenn's heart stopped and he took his first breath of heavenly air. Though we grieve his passing, we grieve mostly for our loss not his gain. But if Glenn were to return and give us one message he would say, 'Prepare to meet your God.'"

Pastor Callahan allowed a few moments to pass before continuing. "Friends, one of these days all of us will die, and it is in this life that we must prepare for that day. Do like Glenn did when one day a few years ago he acknowledged to God that he was a sinner in need of a Savior and he placed his faith in the finished work of Christ to get him to Heaven. That was how he made his preparations by putting his trust in the Lord Jesus Christ. We are not guaranteed a tomorrow. You can trust

Christ where you sit. Don't delay.

For the believer, Glenn would say the same thing, 'prepare.' Live everyday as if it were your last, live it fully and wholeheartedly for the Lord. There is no such thing as wasted time when it is spent in prayer, Bible reading and study, and in sharing your faith. Then, when it's all said and done, you too will have a great send-off celebration like the one being held down here and a great celebration in Heaven. For the Bible says in Psalms 116:15, 'Precious in the sight of the Lord is the death of his saints.'"

He smiled, closed his Bible, and stepped down from the pulpit and asked the congregation for testimonies from those who knew him best. An hour later the line of friends extended down the main isle as people waited to say a good word on behalf of Glenn Tibbits. But as the hour was getting late the pastor gently closed off the testimonial time and led the processional out of the sanctuary and then held a brief graveside committal service.

\*\*\*

Sheriff Conyers returned to the police department and plopped heavily behind his cluttered desk. On top of the stacks of reports lay a copy of the New York Times. Since two of his dearest friends ran the paper, the least he could do was to subscribe to it and read it. Most of the time he enjoyed the commentaries and editorials, this time what he read made his blood boil. The headline top of the fold read: *New York Times* Editor Stan Berkowitz dies in car bombing.

How could this be? Both of his friends were dead, both died violent deaths, both were murdered. The Sheriff knew only what Chase had told him, and he knew enough to get himself killed. *So why sit here in Colorado and wait? I gotta do something and I gotta do something now.*

An hour later, he'd fueled his police cruiser and prepared to drive to Washington, D.C. After a brief meeting with his deputies, he was ready to go, but not without packing a couple of hand-guns, a shot-gun and enough ammunition to start or end a war. As he drove through town, he made one last stop. It was the pastor's house and asked him to get the prayer chain started.

"Bro. Callahan," Conyers said, scuffing the ground nervously, "I'm leaving on very important police business and it would mean a lot to me if I knew that you and the church family were praying for me. I believe that there will be some danger involved and I need God's protection and providential guidance. Would you do that for me?"

A bright smiled broke across the pastor's face. "Sheriff, it would be a privilege to be your prayer support. Why don't we pray right now for you before you go?" The two men prayed and the sheriff left within the hour.

An hour later a black sedan slowly drove through town. It slowed in front of the police department. After circling the small building, it left.

# Chapter Thirteen

The C17 leveled off at thirty thousand feet over the African continent and the occupants of the Lincoln Town Car climbed out and stretched themselves.

Nurse Hodges picked pieces of glass from her hair, ignoring the smudges which marred her features. Chase, on the other hand, was no worse for wear except for his blood soaked shirt; evidence of his recent experience at saving lives. He was checking his disguise in a mirror as one of the security agents interrupted his thoughts.

"Sir, we have wounded men who need your attention."

With a nod, Chase released a tired breath and grabbed his medical kit. He stepped over the cargo netting to a wounded man and knelt down. Nurse Hodges came to his side and handed him his stethoscope.

"You dropped this when you climbed over the car seat," she said with an interesting glint in her eye.

"Thank you Nurse, I don't know what I'd do without this or you for that matter." Then he turned his attention to the wounded man. The young man's shirt was soaked with blood and he was unconscious. By the time he was extracted from the battle zone he was past saving. The voice in his ear-piece confirmed what Chase had determined. Chase moved to the other wounded man. His wounds were not as life-threatening. The medical back-up team talked him through how to treat his wounds and stop the bleeding. It felt good to know that he had made a difference.

As Chase stood and steadied himself, one of the security agents stepped up, "Sir, it's going on noon and we are about an hour behind Air Force One. We are headed to Ramstein Air Base, one of two fully operational air bases left in Germany."

Chase rubbed the back of his neck and looked at the man speaking with him, "How long before we get there?"

He paused and did some quick calculation. "We should get there in about two hours," he said succinctly.

Chase nodded and flexed his fingers realizing that he'd strained his hand when he rescued the president. A moment later, weariness settled over him as a wet blanket, as the adrenalin rush subsided. He trudged to the side of the car and slumped on the front seat. "Well I guess I failed," he muttered without thinking.

"What do you mean you failed?" Nurse Hodges chirped and sat up. She'd been sitting in the back seat resting when Chase got in.

"You didn't fail," she continued, "you were rather heroic in my book," brushing the hair out of her eyes. "You saved the president's life and the remaining security detail from certain death. I'd say that was a pretty good day of work."

He shrugged and looked uncomfortable. "Yes, well I still feel that I could have done more. Look, I'm covered in the

President's blood and who knows what else." Chase said as he looked at his shirt and slacks.

"Well if it means something, I did get this," Nurse Hodges said as she pulled a vial of blood from her pocket.

Chase froze, staring at the tube of blood like a hungry vampire. "What is it, or rather whose is it?" Chase said, eyes bulging.

A bright smile crossed her face. "It's the president's, while you were extracting the shrapnel; I was taking a blood sample. He never even noticed," she said triumphantly.

Chase tried to suppress a grin. "How? I mean why? I mean ..." his voice trailed off.

She looked at him with an impish twinkle in her eyes. "Let's just say we might need it for future reference and leave it at that," and pressed it into his hand with a gentle squeeze.

His mind racing, Chase tried to recollect what was it about her that reminded him of someone else? A distant memory tugged at the fringes of his mind, just out of reach.

Chase sat in the back seat of the car and closed his eyes. He began to pray for Megan and his friends back in Washington. His mind wandered back five and a half years to the early days of when he and Megan both realized that they loved each other. The time spent in the coffee shop had become more than just a time to talk. It had become a time to share their secrets, their dreams, and to bond. Soon their hearts knit as one. It was in Maxine's Diner that Chase asked Megan to marry him. When she said 'yes' the whole diner cheered and celebrated. Because of the rapid pace of Chase's life after the ordeal involving The Order, the marriage planning was pretty simple. A guest preacher was brought in and the sanctuary was decorated with flowers from the only flower shop in town. What few church members were still left and the town's people nearly filled the auditorium to witness the ceremony. After the wedding they had a four-course banquet catered by none other than Maxine's Diner. All in all, it was a wonderful ending to an exciting chapter in both of their lives, and a wonderful beginning to a new chapter.

Now Chase wondered if Megan ever learned of his assignment and if her life was in danger.

Chase's cell vibrated. He looked down at the caller ID, it was Vice President Randall.

"Chase, are you all right?" he asked, his tone echoed with deep concern.

Sitting up, Chase cleared his throat, "Yes, Sir, I am, albeit a bit shaken up."

For a moment static filled his phone. "I've been trying to reach you for days! Where are you? Are you safe? Is this a good time to talk? I can hardly hear over that roaring soun. What's going on?" the vise president asked.

Chase looked around the interior of the mammoth aircraft. "To start with," he said, "the president's motorcade came under attack in Mogadishu and he was wounded."

"Is he going to be okay? I mean, did he survive?" he sounded anxious.

Bryan M. Powell

Chase replayed the conflict in his mind's eye. "Yes, well, an RPG hit the presidential car and he was wounded, I was able to get the shrapnel out and stop the bleeding before he lost consciousness. He will make it. I got him back on Air Force One and they are headed to Ramstein AFB in Germany." He paused to take a swig from a bottle of water. "I left the plane and went back to get the rest of his protective detail. They were still battling it out with the Somalians. It's a good thing I went back. They were just about to be over-run. They piled in the car I was driving and we high-tailed it out of there. Then we caught the C17 on the run. We are now about thirty thousand feet in the air and about forty-five minutes behind them. I am safe, but this is not a good time to talk, I don't know who I can trust."

Again static filled the phone as the signal passed through some interference. "I had no idea," the vice president said. There was an uncomfortable pause in the conversation as each man absorbed the gravity of the situation. "Thank God you were there for the president, I shudder to think what would have happened if he died, even if he is an imposter."

Chase exhaled slowly to keep the tension from taking over. "How about you Mr. Vice President, are you in a safe place?" he asked, glancing around the interior of the aircraft.

Moments stretched. "I'd rather not disclose my whereabouts just yet. You never know who might be picking up this phone call. I fear that I may have endangered your life," the vice president admitted. "I'm so sorry for what I've put you through, maybe I should just turn myself in and face the consequences."

"The consequences?" Chase asked, his voice sounded dry, raspy, yet he continued, "the consequences would be your death and I'm not about to let that happen ... not after what I've just been through. Look, you have got to stay the course Mr. Vice President. You need to ride this one out. We're not out of the game yet, just remember that the fat lady hasn't sung 'till I say sing. Okay?" Chase spoke with a lot more bravado than he was feeling.

Vice President Randall sighed heavily into the phone. "Well you are right, I was just feeling sorry for myself more than for you," he said with growing confidence. "I'll continue my game of hide and seek down here and you keep up the good work on your end Son. Now I'd better get off the phone, I'll call you again in a day or two. Good-bye."

Chase looked at his stethoscope. "Did you guys hear that? Did you get a trace on the origin of the call?" he asked

"Yeah we heard it, but we don't have that kind of technology to trace it," Mr. Tattoo admitted.

"Did you hear that Nurse Hodges got a blood sample?" Chase asked.

The connection crackled as the plane bounced through the tips of some cumulus clouds.

"Yes, and that is great news, now we need that sample analyzed ASAP," said the voice on the other side of the world.

Chase smiled and glanced over his shoulder at his nurse.

"We are about to land at Ramstein AFB and the President may be asking for me."

"Our intel says that he has already landed, picked up another medical team, and is in route for the U.S. as we speak."

Chase cocked his head. "So what are we supposed to do, wait in Germany, or catch the first flight out?"

There was a moment's pause as Mr. Tattoo conferred with his team.

"No, we need that analysis done there in our lab in Germany," Mr. Tattoo said flatly.

"You guys have a lab over here?" Chase asked, his pulse quickening.

"We are a branch of the FBI and we have a field office with a state-of-the-art lab in many countries. Those boys in Germany can be trusted. Now listen carefully as I tell you where to go and who to contact. It won't be a straight line, so listen. Go to the motor pool and commandeer a vehicle. You have enough pull as head of the Presidential medical team to be able to do that. Then, go to Haus des Burger Stadium and go to ticketing, ask for your 'will call' tickets and go to those seats."

Chase shook his head, amazed at how quickly a back-up plan had been assembled. "You said team and tickets, there is only one of me, why are you speaking as if there were two?" looking around the wide body of the air plane.

"Because you need the assistance of Nurse Hodges if you

are to pull this off and survive. When in doubt, follow her lead."

Chase looked across to the other side of the car at his nurse and nodded. "Yes, Sir."

The C17 did a perfect three-point landing and taxied up to the terminal. Before Chase and the others could get themselves unstrapped, members of the military from Ramstein's AFB had gathered at the bottom of the portable stairs. The commanding general and many of his staff had assembled to express their gratitude to Dr. Newberry for saving the President's life.

General Bill Dryden stepped up to Dr. Newberry and saluted him crisply and addressed the team,

"On behalf of a grateful nation and President of the United States of America, I would like to personally thank you and the others for your bravery under extremely difficult circumstances. I have recommended to the President that you and those with you be given a special award for your heroism."

Chase returned his look of determination. "Thank you for your kind words. I am truly humbled by them. I am thankful for the opportunity to serve my president and the men and women who serve with him. I am only saddened that I ... we, could not have saved them all. Unfortunately we had to leave our dead on the field of battle for the angry mob to desecrate," he said as tears welled up in his eyes and ran down his dusty cheek.

"Well Doctor, we have plans for that bunch and there will

be a payback. On that you can rely." His eyes narrowed and a his jaw set. "Now, is there anything, anything I can get for you and your medical team?"

Chase stared at the blood soaked clothes he was wearing, "How about a change of clothes, I seem to be wearing the president's blood, as well as several others."

"Yes, Sir," the General said, "tell you what, I'll get you set up in one of our GHU's, our Guest Housing Units where you can shower, and change. Why don't you then get a good meal, a good night's sleep, and maybe we can squeeze in a tour of this old city before you guys ship out. There's a lot to see."

Chase looked at the others and smiled. "That sounds like a great idea. I think I'll take you up on that. Miss Hodges, how does that sound to you?"

Chase turned and looked at his assistant.

"Yes, Sir. I could use a shower and a good night's sleep as well."

The General smiled genuinely. "Okay then Dr. Newberry, if you will follow Lieutenant Anderson, he will get you squared away." Again he saluted Chase, turned on his heels and retraced his steps.

# Chapter Fourteen

Astrapping young lieutenant stepped up, saluted and said, "Sir, Ma'am, if you will follow me I'll get you squared away."

He guided them to a waiting jeep and took them to guest housing. He handed each of them a set of key cards after unlocking their doors.

"Sir, Ma'am, I hope these accommodations will meet your needs. These are the best we have," he said as he scanned the suite. "Even three and four star generals and their families stay here when they pass through."

Chase took a cursory look around the suite, "Son, this is more than I expected and my thanks goes to the good general."

"Well, then if there is nothing more, here are the keys to the jeep. Breakfast is at six hundred."

Chase coughed into his fist. "I don't think I'll be up by then."

The young lieutenant smiled. "No, I didn't expect you would. We'll be sure to keep a couple plates warm for you. In the meantime, I'll see to it that room-service sends up a hearty meal to each of your rooms, since we've already missed dinner. Oh, and by the way, there is a complete change of clothes for both of you in your closets."

The lieutenant gave them directions to the Officers Mess Hall and then left.

Chase quickly showered and hit the sack. Within a minute he was asleep. The next day was bright and sunny. Rays of morning light shone through the curtains and filled the room. He woke up refreshed and hungry. It was the first good night's sleep he had gotten in the last forty-eight hours and he didn't know when the next one would be. After making a few minor adjustments to his facial and body-wear, he looked into the mirror to make sure everything was in place. The man in the mirror stared back at him with weary eyes. He hoped that no one would notice.

He and Nurse Hodges had decided to meet for breakfast in the Officer's Dining Room around 10:00 a.m. Chase stepped out of his apartment wearing sandals, navy blue slacks and a Hawaiian shirt. Nurse Hodges was already waiting for him in the jeep. She wore a pair of khaki pedal pushers and a white loose fitting blouse and a large sun hat on, which covered most of her head. A pair of sunglasses and a satchel-sized handbag completed the ensemble.

"Good morning Chase, sleep well?" she asked, a bright smile parted her lips.

He nodded. "Like a baby, I slept for a while, woke up, ate something, and went back to sleep." He said with a goofy grin.

Then he started the engine and drove to the Officer's Dining Room for breakfast. As promised, the kitchen staff had prepared two plates containing scrambled eggs, toast, bacon and orange juice. After a heartfelt prayer, thanking God for His protection and leadership, Chase plowed into the meal while Nurse Hodges picked at the eggs. As if on cue, Lieutenant Anderson strode to their table as they finished.

"Sir, Ma'am, I trust you found everything in order and enjoyed your breakfast. For the rest of the day, I am at your service to take you on a sight-seeing tour of Ramstein. I will take you wherever you would like to go. I know all of the major and minor points of interest."

Chase rubbed his hands together and looked at his nurse, then back to the Lieutenant. "Thank you, Sir. I've heard that the Ramstein Stadium is a great place to go, to see a soccer or football game as they call it. Is there a game being played there today?"

A glint of understanding passed between the two men before a word was spoken. "Yes, as a matter of fact there is a game this morning. When will you be ready to go?" Lieutenant Anderson asked.

Chase looked at Nurse Hodges and they both stood to leave. Earlier that morning, Chase's handlers gave him additional instructions to follow and this was where they started.

"We're ready now, let's go," then he paused as he remembered that he had left his medical kit back in the room.

"Oh, hold it just a minute, let me go back to my room and pick up my medical bag. You know what they say, 'Don't leave home without it,'" he explained with a wry smile.

"I've got to get my medical kit as well," Nurse Hodges said, "so I'll be back in a minute too."

The Lieutenant nodded. "Okay then, let's meet back at the front of the Officer's mess in five." With that the three of them parted and reassembled right on time at the side of a waiting Humvee.

"Wow. This is riding in style," Chase exclaimed.

"The ride isn't the best, but it's much safer than that jeep," Lt. Anderson said as he revved up the engine.

Chase took his seat in the front and wondered how they were going to ditch the Lieutenant and not raise a lot of questions. Just about that time his earpiece awoke with the voice of Mr. Tattoo.

"Don't worry about the lieutenant, he's one of us, just follow his instructions."

Chase nodded slightly. *What choice do I have?* Picking up the end of the stethoscope, breathed on it as he were polishing it and smiled ... they got the point.

The Humvee left the safety of Ramstein AFB and headed to the Hauptverkehrsstrade, the inner ring of the sprawling city of Ramstein. They turned left on Landstuhler Street that led them to the stadium area.

As they approached the drop-off area in front of the stadium the lieutenant turned to Dr. Newberry. "Sir, I'm going to drop you off at the ticketing area, and wait for you in the vehicle, we don't like leaving government vehicles unattended in the city. When you have seen enough, just come out of the stadium; I'll be watching for you and pick you up."

Chase thanked the Lieutenant and exited the Humvee with Nurse Hodges close behind.

"Okay, Miss Hodges, am I to assume that you are an FBI agent too?" Chase said as the two of them walked to the ticket booth.

Nurse Hodges hesitated a moment before answering his pointed question. It was obvious by the quizzed look on her face that she hadn't expected the question. "Let's just say that I'm on the side of the good guys and you can call me Rachel when we are in private," she said with a whimsical tone in her voice.

"All right Rachel, where do we go from here?"

"Let's find our seats and our contact will find us and lead us to the next connection. At this time we are functioning on a need to know basis," she said quietly.

Chase had to know ...

"Rachel, are you wearing one of those earpieces too?"

She pulled her hair back revealing a similar device and then smiled.

"Do you hear what I am hearing in that thing?" Chase asked with surprise registering on his face.

She nodded and winked.

They retrieved their tickets and proceeded into the stadium and found their seats. It was a warm day and Chase ordered some soft drinks and popcorn hoping that he could see at least the first quarter of the game before resuming his duties. But that was not to be.

# Chapter Fifteen

A gentle hand touched the president's shoulder. "Mr. President, Mr. President," he roused and then closed his eyes again. He'd slept most of the flight to Ramstein AFB, and then fell back to sleep and slept most of the way back to the United States. It was now around 6 a.m., Monday morning.

"Mr. President, I need to check your vitals now, would you mind sitting up just for a few minutes?" the new medical team assigned to the President had been monitoring his condition, but now needed to check his wound and change the bandages.

As the doctor gingerly lifted the wrapping from around the wound he couldn't help but comment, "The doctor who saved your life did a great job. That piece of shrapnel nearly punctured your spleen, removing it without an x-ray or MRI was like threading a needle blindfolded. This guy was either highly skilled in trauma surgery or very lucky," he said with a look of amazement in his hazel eyes.

The president squinted as the bright light of the sun flowed through the port-hole into the room, "I read his dossier and he seemed to be very competent," the president replied.

An expression of concern crossed the doctor's face as he listened to the president's breathing, "As I examined you, I did notice that you had a place where the doctor drew blood. Do you remember anything about that?"

The president reflected for a moment then shook his head. "No, doc," he said as he scratched his chin thoughtfully, "I was in and out most of the time. The doctor attending me had a nurse at his side, but that's all I remember. Like I said, I was losing a lot of blood, maybe that's where they gave me something for pain or an antibiotic."

In a veiled attempt to mask his concern the doctor shrugged his shoulders. "Well, don't worry about it, you were in the best of hands and I believe you will make a full recovery. Now get some more rest and I'll see you in an hour or so."

The doctor stepped out of the medical clinic and walked down the corridor of Air Force One. He speed dialed someone high in the administration.

"Sir, we have a problem," his tone flat.

\*\*\*

In an apartment located in a run-down section of Washington, D.C. a phone rang.

"Hello?" the Dean asked.

"Have you been able to get anything new from your guest?"

A moment of silence filled the airwaves.

"No, nothing new, I can assure you that we have tried everything short of water boarding."

"You know how vital it is that we get in contact with Mr.

Newton, don't you?" asked the voice on the other end of the connection.

The Dean bristled at being questioned by an underling even though he was high in the administration. "Yes, yes, I don't need to be lectured by a governmental employee. I will keep up the pressure on her, hopefully within the next 24 hours, she will break. By then we should know something."

"Oh, by the way," the caller said cautiously. "You might be interested in knowing that Doctor Newberry drew blood from the president while he was unconscious."

The Dean's eyes narrowed and he hesitated before answering. He spoke slowly so as to let his words sink in. "Now why would Doctor Newberry draw blood from the president?"

The caller considered his words carefully so as to not sound inept.

"Sir, the best we can guess is to have it analyzed, possibly for its DNA." Uncertainty etched his voice.

The muscles in Dean's jaw tightened. "Thank you for that tidbit of information. I will increase the pressure on Mrs. Newton. You do everything in your power to find and eliminate Doctor Newberry. Do you understand?" he seethed.

"Oh yes, absolutely, Sir," said the caller as the line went dead.

The Dean reentered the small dark cell where Megan sat. "Please try again, Mrs. Newton, it is urgent that we get in contact with your husband, and time is running out," the Dean said as he nodded to his assistant.

It was time for a new method of interrogation.

# Chapter Sixteen

he Ramstein Stadium was nearly filled and the game
was about to start when a man approached Chase.

"Doctor," said a man dressed as a soccer coach,
"there is a man with a medical need. Would you mind coming
with me and attending to his needs?"

Chase gave Nurse Hodges a questioning look and rose to
his feet. Nurse Hodges stood and the two excused themselves
and slipped out of the stadium. Without speaking, the man led
them out into the main passage way, which encircled the
stadium. He took an exit which brought them out into the
parking deck. Neither spoke, knowing that the man leading
them was only following the instructions given to him.

Their guide pointed to a black Volvo taxicab parked along
the curb and in his best English said, "Please step into the car
and go with them. Ask no questions, God's speed." He turned
and disappeared into the crowd of passersby.

Rachel looked at Chase, her eyes filled with curiosity.
"That was a comforting thing to say."

"It certainly was, we not only need God's speed, but also
His guidance and protection," Chase replied as he looked out
of the passenger window.

The cab left the stadium area and turned right on

Steinwendener and drove three or four blocks to Stutzenflur Str. As they came to a stop at a Halt sign, a black sedan with its windows darkened pulled alongside of them. One of the windows rolled down and a gun extended from the open window. The blast shattered the window of the vehicle Chase and Rachel were in, but no one was injured. The driver of Chase's car slammed the car into reverse, sped backwards, and made a 180 degree turn and accelerated, leaving the attacker in the distance. A high-speed chase ensued; shots were being fired from the pursuers, most of the time missing their mark.

"Look," Chase said, as he peered out the back window, "a Humvee put itself between us and those guys who are shooting at us."

Rachel raised her head enough to look over the back seat, "Yes and they are returning fire back at the guys in the car," she said between gulps of air.

"Whoever it is, is a pretty good shot; the driver in the pursuing car just got hit," Chase said as they watched the car flip over and burst into flames.

The Humvee slowed and came to a halt as the car Chase and Rachel were in resumed its journey. The driver seemed unperturbed by the diversion. Twenty minutes later the cab came to a stop in front of a ram-shackled building. "Here we are," the cab driver announced. "This is the address I was instructed to take you. Please exit the car and go to that door," he said indicating an unpretentious entry.

"I don't know how you do it, Doc, but you have a way of

attracting attention where ever you go. We think they are on to our little plan and are out to get you," said the voice in Chase's ear. Chase picked up the stethoscope and gave it a questioning look. Then he turned to Rachel for guidance. She nodded for him to comply and they exited the vehicle. They were shaken, but okay, as they cautiously walked up to the front door and knocked. To their surprise, they heard a metallic snap and it eased open. They entered and followed the narrow corridor. After going through several more doors and hallways, they arrived at their destination, a fully operational medical lab.

A tall gentleman in a dark suit stepped up to them, smiled and stuck his hand out. "Welcome to the sovereign nation of the United States of America, Dr. Newberry and Miss Hodges." His voice sounded more like that of John Wayne than an FBI operative.

"I am Robert Gray the department head of this FBI unit here in Ramstein. I trust your journey here was interesting."

The expression on their faces was priceless as Chase gave him a brief summation of their ride.

Agent Gray nodded knowingly. "Yes, we were aware of your little diversion and even anticipated it. We knew someone was monitoring our movements. We just don't know who or why."

Turning to Nurse Hodges, he continued, "I believe you have something of value for me."

The two exchanged glances and Nurse Hodges pulled a vial of blood from her medical kit.

"Is this what you are referring to?" Rachel withdrew a small vial of blood from her handbag.

An interesting glint appeared in Agent Gray's eyes. "Yes, yes it is. Would you mind giving it to me? I would like to give this to the lab boys and let them have a shot at analyzing it. Once we get the DNA broken down we can feed the information to our friends back in the States."

Rachel seemed to deliberate a moment and then handed the small tube to Mr. Gray's extended hand.

He closed his fingers around it and then looked at Chase. "You two have done a great service for your country, and on behalf of Vice President James F. Randall, code name 'cakewalk,' we would like to thank you for you service to your country."

Gray's last statement jolted Chase back to reality. "According to your last statement, you obviously know what we are dealing with."

A look of steel crossed Gray's rugged face. "Yes, Sir, I do and am deeply concerned. From our vantage point there isn't much we in the military can do to remedy the situation in Washington, D.C., but we certainly are glad to help you with your mission. Now, is there anything I can get you?"

Chase stuck his hands onto his pockets and thought for a moment. He was clearly uncomfortable with all this attention. "No, Sir, I don't believe we need anything," he said as he gave Rachel a sideways glance."

She shrugged her shoulders and nodded.

"Would you like to wait for the results?" Agent Gray asked.

"No, Sir," Chase said as he pulled his hands from his pockets and looked at his watch. "Our work is done here. I think we'd better get back to the stadium. Maybe we have time to catch the rest of the soccer game."

Agent Gray smiled and gave him a knowing look. "Very well then, I want to wish you God's speed on your return to the States." He saluted both Chase and Nurse Hodges and Chase snapped to attention and returned the gesture.

Then Agent Gray turned and lifted an envelope and a box from the desk behind him and handed them to Chase. On the outside of the envelope were the instructions; 'Do Not Open until you are airborne.'

"I've been instructed to give you these before you leave. I trust that you will find everything in order, he said as the lieutenant approached.

The driver of the Humvee led them back to his vehicle. As they climbed back into the hummer, the driver looked at Chase with an apologetic look. "I'm sorry to inform you, but the game ended a few minutes ago. We need to be returning to the base."

Chase tugged on his ear thoughtfully as he considered asking for a short tour of the city. He vetoed the idea before pressing the issue. Their ride back to the base was quiet and uneventful. Rachel let out a sigh of relief as they came within sight of the sprawling military base.

The guards at the main gate saluted and signaled for the driver to proceed without being stopped and searched. Rather than going back to the base commander's office, the driver delivered them to his personal residence. General Dryden stepped out of his front door and greeted Chase and Rachel as they exited the hummer. "Well, doctor, I trust you had an enjoyable time in our fair city." He paused but not long enough for Chase to respond.

Then the tone in his voice changed. "However, it looks like your stay will be cut a little short. We have a plane waiting for you as we speak, and they would like it very much if you would board so they can get underway. You might be interested in knowing that plane is loaded with soldiers leaving the Afghanistan war zone and are anxious to get home for a long-awaited leave."

Chase followed the General's gaze as he looked in the direction of the airfield. Then he turned back and nodded.

"Of course General, we would be more than happy to accompany them. Where do we go?" asked Chase respectfully.

The General gave his subordinate a quick nod.

"The lieutenant will see to it that you get to the right plane. I wouldn't want you to fly off in the wrong direction," he said with a whimsical smile. "Again let me say how grateful we all are for your heroic effort on behalf of our nation." Rather than saluting Chase, he stuck out his hand and gripped Chase's firmly.

They reloaded the hummer and the lieutenant drove them

to the far end of the base where the departing planes waited for clearance. He brought the vehicle to a gentle stop next to a jumbo jet.

With a crisp salute, the lieutenant led them to a flight of steps. Following Rachel's lead, they climbed the stairs, entered the mammoth plane. Chase glanced around. The plane was nearly filled with men and women wearing BDU's. Anxiety and weariness filled their eyes as they watched him and Rachel take their seats in First Class. Only then did they relax.

Within twenty minutes the giant plane was lumbering down the runway and lifted off.

"This is a far cry better than the last time we caught a ride on a plane," Rachel said as she kicked off her sandals.

Chase shook his head, "I don't know, I kinda like the way we got on that last plane." A mischievous look danced in his eyes.

Once they were airborne, Chase took out the envelope and carefully opened it. Inside were two new ID's, passports, and money. Instructions also were typed out for each of them to follow. At the bottom of the list of instructions was a hand written note to Chase. It was written from Mr. Tattoo.

"Chase, I don't want you to worry, we are doing everything in our power, but your wife has been abducted," the note read.

"Abducted! My wife has been abducted? How could that be?" His outburst jolted dozens of battle weary, home-sick solders to the reality that no one was safe, even in America.

The news shocked them like an incoming round.

"I thought that the FBI sent an agent by to be her personal bodyguard," said Rachel with a look of concern on her face.

"Quiet you idiot, you want to get the whole plane load of soldiers up in arms?" said the unknown voice in his ear piece.

Just then Chase looked around him and saw every eye in the plane staring at him. Soldiers from all branches and ranks were sitting there ready to go and search for this stranger's missing wife. The only thing stopping them was about thirty thousand feet of empty air space. He gulped and smiled sheepishly and sat back down.

"Somebody has abducted my wife and you didn't tell me?" Chase said as he looked at his stethoscope.

The voice came back, "Sorry Chase, we couldn't tell you for fear of compromising the mission, but let me assure you that we are doing everything in our power to locate your wife."

Rachel placed her hand on Chase's arm and gave it a gentle squeeze. "Oh Chase, I am so sorry."

Chase's head jerked up as if pulled by a rope.

"You just called me Chase, no one but a very few people even know who I am and you just blurted out my real name for the whole plane to hear. Who are you anyway?" he eyed her suspiciously. All of a sudden, it clicked, "You're not Rachel or Nurse Hodges, you're Jennifer, aren't you?"

She hesitated a moment then nodded and smiled. "I wouldn't have recognized you had I not been told in advance."

A wave of mixed emotions swept over Chase. He was glad

to have Jennifer at his side, but a tinge of guilt also pricked his heart. And then his thoughts turned to his wife. "They got M, Jennifer, they got my wife." Tears welled in his eyes.

"I know, I'm so sorry Chase," she said, pain edging her voice.

There was an uncomfortable pause in the conversation. Then Chase looked over at Jennifer. "It never even dawned on me that it was you. I didn't recognize you at all." Jennifer brushed a few strands of hair behind her ear.

"Yeah, those guys back at the tattoo shop can work miracles," she said as she looked at herself in the reflection of a window.

Chase scratched his neck. "Do you mean that they sent you to the same dingy tattoo shop as they sent me? What do you think of Mr. Ta—"

The look on Jennifer's face reminded him that their every word was being monitored back at the tattoo shop.

A moment later Chase's phone vibrated, he looked at the caller ID.

It was Megan.

# Chapter Seventeen

The sight of the Washington, D.C. skyline was a bit intimidating as Sheriff Conyers entered the first mix-master. The traffic, the smog and the crush of people was more than he had expected. He had been driving nearly non-stop from Beaumont to Washington, D.C. and though he was road weary, he was ready for action. The only problem was that in a city this big, he had no idea where to begin.

His deputy had called him earlier in the day and told him that a strange vehicle had been roaming the streets. It was obvious that someone was looking for him and he was glad he left when he did. But now he had to focus on his mission. To his thinking, the best place to begin was to start by circling *The New York Times* building hoping to catch a glimpse of someone he knew. So he nosed his cruiser in the direction of the downtown area. Unfortunately for him, it was rush hour and since he didn't know the area, he got turned around and ended up on a one-way street going the wrong way. It wasn't long before the Sheriff was good and lost. So he drove over to a tree lined park and stopped along the curb and prayed! His was a simple prayer from a heart of simple faith.

"Lord, I'm not as lost as I once was, but I'm as lost as a man can get in this big place. Would you lead me to where I can do the most good? In Jesus' name, Amen."

While he waited, he fell asleep. How long he slept he didn't know. It was at least the rest of that day and all though the night. Saturday morning Sheriff Conyers woke up hungry and with a sense of mission. He pulled out into traffic and looked for the first diner with a crowd of police cars and firemen. He found just what he was looking for and went in, ordered his favorite, steak and eggs. Since he was in uniform, albeit that of a small mid-west town, he attracted a crowd of policemen all questioning his authenticity. After producing all the proper documentation for wearing a sheriff's badge and sidearm, the men settled down and he was able to enjoy the company of his fellow officers. As a part of his conversation, Sheriff Conyers told the men in the diner that he was looking for a friend of his, Chase Newton, the reporter. To many of them his name was a household word.

Conyers leaned forward and put his elbows on the table, "Look fellas, if you should find him, let me know by calling me on my cell phone. And if I find him or if I happen to need your help, how can I reach all of you?"

The captain of the local precinct, a man with sandy colored hair and a young face, spoke up as he reached into his pocket and produced a small card with his cell number written on it. "Look sheriff, just call me and I'll get the word out in a hurry."

Sheriff Conyers smiled and thanked his new friends profusely. "Hey, by the way, I was wondering if there are some good places where I could do a little sightseeing while

I'm here."

He got a bevy of answers as each man called out his favorite historical site. The captain spoke up and mentioned the Lincoln Memorial or the Vietnam War Memorial. Another burly officer stepped up to Conyers and placed his beefy hand on his shoulder. "You look like a Navy man, Sheriff, I'd bet you would enjoy visiting the Vice President's residence on Observatory Circle." He told the sheriff that this old estate dates back to 1893. Located on the northeast grounds of the U.S. Naval Observatory, the house was built for its superintendent. "It's a grand old place and you'll love it," he said with the pride of an old Navy man.

"Thanks a lot. I am an old Navy man, as you guessed, and just might go there," the sheriff said politely.

***

As a result of the assassination and attempt on his life, Vice President Randall went into hiding in a nearby hotel. He knew he couldn't stay there long, so he came up with a plan. He exchanged his street clothes for his personal bodyguard's, and slipped back into his personal residence on Observation Circle, under the cover of darkness.

With his security detail beefed up he felt he was relatively safe. Plus, everyone on the compound was sequestered, absolutely no one was to communicate with the outside and no one was to leave the property. Everyone was more than glad to comply, knowing that the fate of the country hung in the balance. His home became a fortress under siege. The head of his security detail unlocked the small arsenal of weapons stashed in the basement and distributed them to all the staff from the secretaries down to the cooks. Then he gave them a crash course on how to use the weapon. He just hoped that the incoming V.P. wouldn't need the residence for a few more weeks.

While preparations were being made for his protection, Vice President Randall picked up his phone and tried Chase's cell phone again. It rang.

# Chapter Eighteen

" "Hello, Megan?" Chase said tentatively. "Chase, I'm ...

The phone was ripped from her trembling hand.

"Mr. Newton," The Dean said, interrupting Megan mid-sentence, "so good to talk with you. I believe we have a guest with us who would love very much to speak with you, but first we have a little business to transact." He eyed Megan lustfully as he spoke.

"By the way I have not had the honor of meeting you personally, but you may remember one of my protégées, Pastor T. J. Richards?"

Chase's pulse quickened at the mention of that name and he caught himself not breathing. "Who are you and what do you want with me?" He finally asked through clinched teeth.

"Oh, yes, my name is unimportant," he said with the wave of his hand, "but for the record, they call me 'Dean,' or 'The Dean' because I spent so many years in the education business training young impressionable minds to think on a higher plane. But I digress; I still have not gotten over the way you spoke to T. J. at your last meeting. I plan to rectify that when we meet." His voice turned to a sneer.

Chase lost no time in making his demands known. "What are you doing with my wife? Why have you taken her? She's done nothing and knows nothing; let her go." Chase demanded while Jennifer sat wide eyed.

"All in good time, all in good time, but first I have a proposition for you." The Dean calmly replied, he paused to let the tension build. "You tell me where your Mr. Randall is and your wife will live to see another day. If not, her life will end suddenly and violently, do you understand?" The Dean paced back and forth as he spoke.

Chase clutched the arm of his chair as he tried desperately to control his emotions. "I don't know where the vice president is, I have only spoken with him a few times since the assassination attempt," he said as he desperately tried to assess the situation.

"Then you had better find out where he is or," he paused for effect, "or your wife dies," The Dean let his voice trail off.

Emotion constricted Chase's throat. Blinded by anger, he was at a total loss for words. Jennifer tried to console him but he was at his wits end. He needed a miracle and fast.

The Dean continued his verbal onslaught. "I understand you took something from the president, I wonder if you could tell me what it was?" His tone took on a sinister ring.

Chase's mind raced. "What are you talking about? I saved the president's life for crying out loud."

In the background the sharp report of a weapon being fired, sent a burst of adrenaline through his veins like ice crystals. "What was that?" Chase demanded, trying to keep his voice level. Visions of his dead wife flashed across his mind.

"Oh, so sorry," The Dean said nonchalantly, "my gun has a hair trigger and accidentally discharged, but I think it missed her. Let's see, yes, she is still breathing. Now you were saying?" he paused, "Yes, you were about to tell me what you took from the president and for what purpose."

Feeling defeated at the game of cat and mouse, Chase finally admitted he'd taken a sample of the president's blood in order to get a DNA analysis.

"What will that prove, you fool? When the old Mr. Randall is dead and gone there will be nothing to compare it to. It will make no difference and all of your pathetic efforts will be in vain." He said triumphantly. "It is Monday, 7:00 a.m., Eastern Standard Time, now find the Vice President within the next 48 hours, or your wife dies," he said vehemently and the phone went dead.

The look on Jennifer's face said it all.

"Did you guys get all that?" Chase asked. "We got big problems and I need your help big time."

"Yes Chase, we heard," said Mr. Tattoo, "and we're on it. We have our best people working all their sources. It won't be long before we get a lead on her. By the way, the police found our operative a few days ago in her car. She'd been shot in the head. Someone must have slipped a bug inside Stan's office before he discovered the one in his lampshade."

Chase closed his eyes and thought back to a week ago.

"There was a man coming out of Glenn's office the day I broke the news to him. His name is Senator Max Wilcox. He had to have planted the bug."

"Then these guys were on to us from the get-go," Mr. Tattoo said as his chair squeaked.

"But they don't know where the vice president is, at least not yet," Chase reiterated as he rubbed his forehead. By now a tension headache was bearing down on him.

Mr. Tattoo sighed heavily. "Yeah, but they got your wife and they want you to lead them right to him. Oh, and by the way, they will probably kill you and your wife as an extra bonus."

"I know, I know, said Chase, weariness seeping into his voice. "I've already taken that into consideration. If we get into a worst case scenario, we are ready to meet the Lord, but I just hate the idea of jeopardizing the life of the vice president or anyone else."

As he spoke, his cell phone began to vibrate. Looking at the caller ID, he breathed a prayer of thanksgiving. "Look, I gotta take this call, it's the vice president." Chase held his phone in front of him and pushed the call button. "Hello Mr. Vice President"

The voice on the other end of the line said, "code word 'cakewalk.'"

Chase answered succinctly, "crosswalk."

"Is this a good time to talk?" the Vice President asked.

Chase looked around the cabin of the giant plane with a tense smile.

"Yes, Mr. Vice President, it is a very good time to talk.

I'm on a plane from Ramstein AFB, loaded with soldiers coming out of Iraq and Afghanistan." Keeping his voice to a whisper, "But Sir, I, or rather, we have a huge problem."

"Oh? What's new? Tell me about it, Son," Chase could tell by his voice that Randall was truly moved by his situation.

"Well, first of all, I just got a call from a man calling himself The Dean and he informed me that he and his henchmen abducted my wife. They are demanding I lead them to wherever you are. Next, I just found out Stan's office was bugged the day I went in and broke the story to him. They know about Dr. Cleve Newberry and his nurse taking a sample of the president's blood to have a DNA analysis done on it. They've given me 48 hours to turn you over or my wife dies." Chase tried to keep his tone respectful.

The drone of the jet's engines drowned out the uncomfortable pause.

"Well, we can't let that happen, can we. Look, I have some documentation to prove that laws were broken, that foreign influences and agents have infiltrated our government. Some of those people who sit in very high places are not even citizens of the United States. We will have to be very careful, however, who we talk with. I know of several people who can help us, but we must act fast." His voice carried a tone of determination in it and Chase was encouraged.

If this man ever makes it to the Presidency, he will make a good one, he thought.

Chase put the phone on speaker so Jennifer could hear the

conversation between him and Vice President Randall. She was clearly interested in finding Megan and saving the life of the man she heard speaking on the phone.

"You said documentation and that reminded me of something. Before Glenn died, he told me to check his laptop because he had a lot of information that could be used to uncover this plot."

"Where is the laptop now?" Randall asked, his voice curling up in the form of a question.

"It's in the SUV I rented and left back in D.C."

The vice president cleared his throat. "Can you get to it?"

Chase's mind pictured the SUV sitting where he left it with a bomb strapped to its underbelly. "It's too risky even disguised as Dr. Newberry. They probably followed my paper trail and are watching the car around the clock. Either that or they have placed a bomb under it. I don't think they know about the laptop," Chase said, as clouds whisked past his window.

By now few, if anyone, was interested in the low conversation Chase was having with the man on the phone. They were either sleeping or watching the on-board movie.

Jennifer leaned in close to the phone. "Mr. Vice President, this is Jennifer aka Rachel Hodges, Dr. Newberry's nurse assistant, we need to get a DNA sample from you so that the lab boys can do an analysis and comparison. How do you propose that we do that?"

There was a slight pause as Vice President Randall thought

about his options. Then he spoke with determination. "Despite the risks, we are going to have to meet somewhere. I'll give you a blood sample and whatever information I have. With what you have on Glenn's laptop, you should have the upper hand on this bunch."

Jennifer leaned back and let Chase take the lead again. "We know who they are. They call themselves, The Order. We have had dealings with them over four years ago with that Document thing. Do you remember?

"Oh yes, I remember. I was not involved, but I followed the events closely. Back then I was just a junior Senator of the minority party, barely noticed by the guys running the White House or the Congress for that matter. After you broke the story, I was on one of the committees investigating that bunch. I too am quite aware of The Order."

"Then you know they can not to be taken lightly. They have killed once and will do it again when they feel threatened," Chase said with weariness in his voice. "Right now you and I are a big threat to them."

"Up until recently I have been getting daily briefs on the movements of The Order, but now I am beginning to think that the information they were giving me was flawed," the vice president's tone darkened.

"Knowing what I now know, you're probably right." Chase rubbed the back of his neck. His migraine was bearing down on him like a locomotive.

"What time do they expect you to land?" the vice president

inquired.

Jennifer noticed that Chase needed some relief. She brushed her hair back and leaned into the phone. "We should be landing at Dulles within the hour. Look, we know they will be looking for us so we are going to have to change identities before we deplane or they will capture us right off the bat. After we get out of the airport we'll rent a car using Chase's new identity. After that we'll have to plan our next move."

Chase leaned back in his seat and closed his eyes hoping for some relief from the pain he was feeling when another call beeped in. He opened his blood-shot eyes and looked at the caller ID. "Look, Mr. Vice President, I've got an incoming call and it might be Megan, I need to take it."

As Chase fielded the incoming call, Jennifer excused herself and made her way to one of the stewardesses and requested some extra strength aspirin for her partner. In a moment she returned with the pain medication and a bottle of water, which Chase gladly received.

"Okay, I'll get off the phone, again let me say thank you for all that you have done and will do."

The call ended and Chase pushed the green button.

"Hello?" Chase said, expecting to hear Megan's voice.

"Chase is that you?" It was Sheriff Conyers.

"I just thought I'd try your cell one more time. Man, I've been driving around this city for what seems like days looking for you. Where are you?" Frustration tinged the sheriff's voice.

Chase glanced over at Jennifer and gave her a confused

look. "Sheriff, what city are you talking about? You're not talking about Beaumont are you?"

"No, I'm in Washington, D.C." his voice tightened.

Chase felt heat creeping up his neck. "Washington, D.C." he repeated. "How'd you get there?"

Without missing a beat Sheriff Conyers continued, "I drove here like you did. I've been looking all over this place for you. Where are you?" he asked as he swerved around a corner and found an empty parking slot. He brought the police cruiser to an abrupt halt and listened.

Chase was incredulous. "I'm in a plane, and I'm about an hour out from Dulles International Airport."

"A plane." he echoed. "Why are you on an airplane?" Now it was Sheriff Conyers' turn to be surprised.

"Look, I'll fill you in on all that when I see you. Right now my phone battery is running low. Could you be waiting in your car in the 'Arrival' pick-up area?"

"Yeah sure," attempting to sound agreeable.

"Now I need to warn you, I don't look like myself." Chase observed as he took a quick peek at Jennifer.

"Oh! Is that right? Who will you look like?"

"When you get here, look for two people dressed as tourists with colorful hats and sunglasses. Oh, and by the way, they are a mixed couple," he said as he gave Jennifer a mischievous look.

"A mixed couple, what do ya mean by that?"

"You know, a black man and a white lady, that kind of

mixed couple," Chase said with a smile in his voice.

"Oh, that kind, I get it. Who are you with any way?"

Not wanting to say too much, nor blow her cover, Chase opted to keep the good Sheriff guessing. "Let's just say she's a very good friend of yours."

Releasing a frustrated sigh, "I can't wait to meet her. I'll be waiting for you," the sheriff said and he ended the conversation.

# Chapter Nineteen

arlier in the day Chase and Jennifer opened the box and found a couple of Hawaiian shirts and large brimmed hats. Underneath the hats was several hundred dollars in cash, new credit cards and driver's licenses. Chase was amused as he inspected his new apparel.

"I guess the more attention you draw to yourself the less likely you are to be seen," Jennifer said holding up her new flower covered blouse. They each took turns going to the airplane's rest room and changing cloths. By the time the plane arrived at Dulles International Airport, Dr. Newberry and Nurse Hodges didn't exist any longer and a lovely couple from Jamaica emerged from the plane.

Using a new GPS, which he purchased from a local electronics shop, Sheriff Conyers had no difficulty in finding his way to Dulles International Airport. He pulled up to the curb marked 'No Parking' and waited. When a police officer approached his car, he simply showed him his badge and the officer saluted him and left. Within a half hour a couple, carrying no luggage, stepped out of the terminal and looked around. The sheriff flashed his lights and the couple from Jamaica slowly made their way over to his car. Although there were lookouts, no one noticed the mixed couple in colorful shirts as they got into the police cruiser. Conyers put the car in gear and slowly pulled away from the curb.

After they cleared the airport parking area they all breathed a collective sigh of relief. Chase broke the tense silence. "You did good, Mr. Sheriff, sur!"

Shocked, the sheriff swerved nearly hitting the shoulder of the road as he look at Chase. "Chase is that you? I'd never recognize you or Miss Jennifer."

A wide grin spread across Chase's dark skin. "That's the plan," Chase said. "Do you think that anybody spotted us?"

Conyers glanced in his rear-view mirror before answering, "I doubt it, you just blended in like all the other people dressed weird," the sheriff said with a smile.

"Weird, I'll have you know that this shirt cost two bucks at the Good Will Thrift shop," a voice said in Chase's ear piece.

Chase deliberated a moment, and tried to think of a pithy comeback, but instead chose to ignore the comment.

As they passed through yet another congested intersection, Sheriff Conyers gave a quick glance at Chase. Do you have any idea where we are going? I sure could use a little guidance."

Chase leaned over the front seat and spoke to the Sheriff, "Yes, we need to go someplace safe and do some quick planning. The vice president will be calling me within the hour and I need to tell him what the next move is."

Conyers gave him a big grin. "I know of the perfect place. It's the diner where I had breakfast. We just might be able to get some reinforcements while we're there too." Then he nosed the car into traffic and headed to the diner. With his new GPS giving him directions, he made the journey without once missing a turn. As he turned into the parking lot and applied pressure to the brake as he guided the police cruiser into an empty parking slot. He then reached over and patted his new toy on its top. "This is the first time to my knowledge that a woman had a better sense of directions than I did."

Jennifer rolled her eyes and shook her head in a typical female fashion.

Upon arriving at the diner, the Sheriff suggested that he go in and scope out the place first. He came back with the all clear sign and Chase accompanied by Jennifer made their way into the diner.

The lunch crowd had thinned out, leaving a few police officers finishing up on the house specialty, apple pie al a mode. To one side there were some county workers, but other than that the trio had the place to themselves.

At Chase's behest they pushed their way further into the small seating area. "Let's sit in the back and face the entrance."

A friendly waitress greeted them, but took a special interest in the sheriff. She made sure that his coffee cup was never less than half empty and she was more than willing to dominate the conversation if it involved talking to him. It was obvious to Chase and Jennifer that she must have been a very lonely woman, though it probably hadn't occurred to the good sheriff. Finally, to the relief of Chase and Jennifer, the friendly waitress moved on to other patrons and left them alone. Over lunch Chase filled the sheriff in on all that had happened and the sheriff shared all that happened in Beaumont and in the diner earlier.

Once they were all up to speed, Chase got serious. "Look Sheriff, I have got to get to the SUV I rented a few days ago, but I know it will be watched. How do you propose we go about getting it?"

Conyers took a swig of coffee before answering, then he looked at Chase with a whimsical smile. "That's simple Chase, I'm a police officer responding to a report of a stolen vehicle, and I might add that according to the car rental office it is stolen and you are wanted for grand auto theft."

A look of surprise swept over Chase's weary face. "Great, now I can add that to the list of things I wanted for; stealing an SUV."

Conyers gave Jennifer a wink and broke out in laughter at the sight of seeing his friend squirm a little. "That's okay. I think I can work things out with the rental company since it's your first offense. Now where's the car parked, Chase?" He asked with raised eyebrows.

Chase rubbed the back of his neck nervously as he tried to remember where it was that he left the car. "It's in a parking garage at Eleventh and Clifton Street. But be careful, there could be a car bomb, or someone could be sitting in a nearby car waiting to shoot whoever comes near that car."

Conyers leaned his elbows on the table as his waitress friend approached with a fresh pot of coffee. "Well, before I go and get my head blown off I think I'll call in a favor." Then he reached into his uniform pocket and pulled out the card given to him by the young precinct captain. He dialed the number and waited.

"Hello Captain, this is Sheriff Conyers, I gotta favor to ask of you. Could you send a bomb squad to the parking garage at the end of Eleventh and Clifton Street? There's an SUV sitting there and I got a hunch that there just might be a bomb underneath it."

That brought the captain's feet to the floor as he sat watching a ball-game on the television. "If there's another bomb threat, I need to get my team on to it now. I'll send my Bomb Squad out there A.S.A.P. Thanks for the heads up, Sheriff."

Conyers smiled. "Great, I'll meet you there," then he closed his phone and looked at Chase triumphantly.

Chase's fell open and he shook his head in amazement.

"You sure get connected fast around here, don't you sheriff?" Jennifer said as she watched the waitress warily.

Conyers nodded at the overly friendly waitress. "Well it's not always what you know," Conyers said proudly, "but who you know in this city." Then he handed a generous tip to the waitress.

# Chapter Twenty

In a city as troubled as Washington, D.C. it's not unusual to see Fire and Emergency vehicles responding to a call. The sound of sirens has become a part of the everyday fabric of life. So when the Bomb Squad raced through the city streets, no one took much notice. When they arrived, the first thing the courageous men and women did was cordon off the area.

Yellow police tape greeted Sheriff Conyers as he neared the parking garage. He watched a team of skilled men maneuver what looked like a toy truck; actually it was a remote bomb sniffing vehicle into position. It wasn't long before they found what they were looking for.

"There it is," said the squad leaded to Conyers. "It's a good thing you didn't go barging up to that SUV of yours. You would have been blown to smithereens. Give the boys a few minutes and they'll have that thing disarmed and we will take the vehicle to the police barn where we will go over it with a fine-tooth comb looking for fingerprints." His voice was calm but pierced with a noticeable trace of tenseness.

As they turned to leave, Sheriff Conyers leaned close. "Look Captain, I believe that there is some important evidence inside that SUV I need for an ongoing investigation. Before you take off with it, could I check it out?" The captain glanced up from his paperwork, his eyes narrowed for a moment as he thought through the request.

With a nod, he said, "Yes of course. But wear a pair of rubber gloves. I don't want the evidence contaminated by any foreign fingerprints."

Conyers relaxed and gave him a big smile. "Sure thing Captain," he said as he pulled on a pair of latex gloves.

Even though he knew it was safe, still he approached the SUV with caution. He opened the passenger side door and carefully removed the laptop, thanked the Captain and returned to the diner.

While Conyers was retrieving the laptop, Chase and Jennifer were catching up on each other's lives. Chase told her about his wedding. She listened intently. Then they filled in the remaining time with small talk. Conyers entered the diner to the delight of the waitress who seemed to have claimed him as her own. But rather than letting her distract him, he made a bee-line to the table where Chase and Jennifer were sitting.

"You better be glad you didn't try to go somewhere in that SUV, you would have been blown to pieces. Here's the laptop." He said as he eyed the waitress, "how about we go down to the local police precinct and check it out? I'll feel much safer in that kind of environment."

Jennifer, who was growing increasingly anxious, was more than happy to get out of the diner. Chase nodded and the three of them quickly agreed. Again Conyers left a sizable tip as he paid the bill, took the receipt, stuffed it into his pocket and led the group out to his waiting cruiser. Using his GPS, he was able to find his way to the nearest police precinct. The officer greeted the Sheriff and directed him and the others to a private workspace where they could log on to the internet. Within a few minutes they were looking at the mother-load of very damaging documents.

Conyers let out a low whistle as he stared at the screen. "This stuff implicates the President, Senator Max Wilcox, a sitting Supreme Court judge, a Secretary of the Treasury, the justice of the Sixth District Court of Appeals, and several Senators."

"Look here," Jennifer pointed to a sidebar, "there are links to the money source and off-shore banking accounts. It looks like this conspiracy goes up to the highest seats in our government."

Jennifer stood and started pacing the floor. "I knew Dad was working on something very important since he retired from the agency, but this is big, really big."

"Yeah, and it probably got him killed too," the Sheriff said, not realizing that he had failed to tell Jennifer that her father had been killed back in Beaumont.

Jennifer's eyes went wide. "Did you say that my Dad is dead?" Tears welled up in her eyes and she began to sob.

Realizing his oversight Conyers wrapped his burly arms around Jennifer in a fatherly fashion and embraced her. "Oh Jennifer, I'm so sorry. I didn't realize that no one had told you that your father was dea…" he let his voice trail off. After an uncomfortable silence he continued, "I had no idea that you didn't know." Then he gave Chase a questioning look as if to say why haven't you told her?

Through tearstained eyes Jennifer looked at Chase and asked, "Did you know too Chase?"

Chase's gaze dropped to the floor as he had to admit his oversight. "Yes, I knew, but couldn't tell you before now. It was just recently that I even found out who you were," he said in his defense.

"You knew and didn't tell me!" Her words pierced his heart like a lance.

Chase knew she was angry and hurting.

"I'm so sorry, Jennifer, I'm so sorry," his voice thick with emotion. He was grieving the loss of his friend.

Silence reigned for the next several minutes until Jennifer regained her composure. Finally, she reached down and picked up her overstuffed purse and rooted around in it until she found a pack of tissues. She wiped her eyes and attempted to act normal, but Chase could tell she had erected a wall around her heart. It was there maybe to keep the pain in or keep people out … him out. He couldn't tell.

Finally, Jennifer spoke, her voice barely above a whisper. "I knew in my heart of hearts that probably that's the way Dad would go. He lived passionately for two things: His God and his country. I hope he finished well for both of them."

By then both men were stealing tissues from her. They

gave each other enough space and time to regain their composure before moving forward.

Finally Chase spoke, "If it's any consolation, I can say that he did," he paused a moment to clear his throat. "I was there when it happened; he gave his life serving the country he loved. And Jennifer, I know that he had the peace of God that passes all understanding when he crossed over into God's presence," Chase added, his voice softening.

Jennifer took a halting breath. "That's a comfort to know."

"How did it happen anyway?" Jennifer finally asked after a few moments.

"Stan sent me to confer with your dad and to fill him in on the latest developments with the vice president. We met at the old diner for breakfast before heading out to his favorite fishing hole. He brought along this laptop with all these files. We hoped we could figure out a way to save the vice president's life and at the same time blow the cover on what's going on in D.C. He never got a chance. We were just getting started when a sniper got him in his cross-hairs. The bullet must have pierced his aorta. He didn't last a minute after he was hit. But before he died, he told be the password to this file, it was painful to see him bleed out and not be able to do a thing about it."

Chase and the others just sat there staring at the computer until the sheriff finely cleared his throat and wiped the tears from his eyes and looked at Jennifer. "I will admit we had a really great funeral service for your dad. He would have been embarrassed by all the kind words the people of the church and town said about him. He'll probably go down as a local hero or something. Heck, they just might put a statue in the center of the town square in his honor," he added to lighten the mood.

"Guys, let's pray right now," Chase said. "We need God's peace, protection, and providential guidance big time."

They prayed and as their prayer time ended Chase's cell phone vibrated again.

It was the President of the United States of America.

# Chapter Twenty-One

Vice President Randall had not been idle, neither had his staff. Since arriving at the Naval Observatory, they had been working for hours planning his escape from his residence, planning how to get the incriminating evidence into the hands of the right people. Their options were rather thin. The evidence implicated many and there were only a few people in the government who had not been compromised. Of them were the Secretary of State, the Secretary of Defense and the Secretary of Homeland Security. How many of their subordinates who couldn't be trusted was not known. His notes did not say. He also knew that the Justice of District Court of Appeals in Washington, D.C. was not compromised, and so a plan began to emerge, but how to implement it was the problem.

With the Naval Observatory located along a mile from the Potomac River, the plan was to get the vice president to Rock Creek, an estuary feeding the Potomac, put him in a small speedboat, and take him to a nearby Yacht Club. Then take a taxi to the steps of the Supreme Court where he would meet with Chase and make the exchange. But his chief of security was dubious.

"Well Carl, now that you have reviewed my plan what do

you think?" Vice President Randall asked.

He looked up skeptically and answered without hesitation. "Mr. Vice President, this plan of yours is very risky and has several flaws in it," said the head of his security detail.

The vice president glanced up from the sheet of paper he was holding. "Oh? How so?"

His friend Carl, the head of security, took a seat directly in front of him and scanned the face of the man he was sworn to protect. "Well for starters, what if someone is watching the compound, or the riverside. You would be a sitting duck."

Then Randall rubbed his weary eyes and considered his statement. "Okay, let's step back and rethink this whole plan. Then I'll call Chase."

After an hour of hashing it out, he dialed Chase's number … the cell phone was busy.

Once again, Chase's phone rang.

"Hello." Chase said expecting to hear from the vice president.

"Dr. Newberry, you've been a busy man," The president tone sounded overly friendly.

Chase froze, his mind reeling.

"Now before we get down to the real reason for my call, let me express my appreciation and the gratitude of this nation for your heroism. You not only saved my life, but a number of your countrymen in the face of certain death and I am personally grateful." The president paused as he segued to a more sober tone of voice.

"However, it's too bad that you will not enjoy the fruits of your labor," he paused and allowed time for Chase to follow his line of reasoning. "It seems that while I was incapacitated you performed a medical procedure, which I would not have approved had I been of sound mind. You violated the law and your oath of office. It gives me great sadness to inform you that you won't be serving on my medical detail any longer." He paused, and Chase heard him take a sip of water.

"As a matter of fact, I need you to turn yourself over to the authorities without delay. If you do so immediately I will personally go to bat for you and see to it that those nasty charges could be dropped. If not, you will be apprehended and tried for treason. You see, we know what you are up to and we are prepared to go to whatever lengths we need to, to put a halt to this foolish and harebrained idea of yours." The president let the import of his statements press in upon Chase's mind.

All Chase could think of saying in response was. "How in the world did you get this cell number?"

A wicked laugh percolated through the connection. "Oh Doctor, if you are a Doctor that was easy," he said without answering his question.

"But now listen, we have someone of great value to you and if you would be so kind as to let us know the location of the man who is impersonating me, then we can resolve this whole mess quickly and quietly and you will be given the honors you so rightly deserve. And I might add, have your wife returned to you. You see we have been monitoring your movements and know what you are attempting to do, but it will never work. It is now 1:00 p.m. and if I am correct you are down to about thirty-six hours before the 'dead-line' is up that my colleague gave you. 'Time is running out."

\*\*\*

As Chase released a frustrated sigh, his phone vibrated again. It was another call, but his battery was running low. He took the call anyway.

"Hello?" his asked, voice turning grim.

Without any preliminaries the vice president began speaking, "Chase, I've got a plan on how we can meet. Listen carefully and take this down." he waited to give Chase time to get a pencil and paper. "Okay are you ready? I need you to rent a speedboat from the Washington Harbor and make your way up Rock Creek. It is a fairly large estuary that feeds into the Potomac.

You can get all the way to Montrose Park by way of Rock Creek.

The Charles C. Glover Bridge crosses over the creek at one point, I'll meet you under the bridge. We can make the exchange there. Then you head back down Rock Creek until you get to the Potomac River and take it to the Tidal Basin. Land the boat at one of the docks and make your way up to the street level. There will be a taxi waiting for you. Take it from Fourteenth Street to Pennsylvania Ave. Turn right and go to the corner of Pennsylvania Ave. and Ninth Street."

Sheriff Conyers and Jennifer leaned in closer and listened

attentively as the Vice President spoke.

"What's there?" Chase interrupted.

"That's where the J. Edger Hoover FBI Building is located. There will be someone inside who will be watching for you. Go with him and do what he says.

Chase cast a searching stare at the two people who he could trust with his life. The tension was palpable but his thoughts were broken as Randall continued.

"I think it best that you come here under the cover of darkness. It will be a lot harder to see where you are going, but you will avoid anyone who might be watching this place. There is a small dock along that stretch of river and there will be a red light on the boat dock as you approach from the south. Can you do that?"

The three considered his words for a minute before nodding in agreement.

"Yes, Sir, but I've got to tell you, this is very risky," Chase said as he read the worried faces of his compatriots. "I just got off the phone with the president asking me, rather he was demanding me, to turn myself in and tell him your whereabouts in exchange for my wife."

It was as if the vice president was standing in the room; his voice had an edge of steel in, and Chase could feel a set of cold blue eyes bearing down upon him. "Look Chase, we've got to put them on defense rather than on offense. Right now they are controlling events, but if we can get this damaging information into the right hands, we can turn this thing around.

I'll give you a blood sample and the evidence. Then you hightail it over to the FBI lab and let them do the DNA analysis. In the meantime I'll be getting those who are still loyal to the Constitution lined up to assemble on the Supreme Courts steps and demand an investigation into allegations of fraud and treason by this administration. I know that bunch; they will be thrown into a defensive mode. They'll start circling the wagons, and closing ranks. They will immediately begin a smear campaign against me and those Senators and Cabinet Heads who choose to stand against them. They will be so busy doing that, that we should be able to get to the New York Times and substantiate our evidence."

There was a beep from his phone indicating that the battery was about to give out. "That sure sounds like a plan, but without God's divine help we will fail. There are so many evil man in high places, it just seems an impossible task," Chase said, his voice tinged with pain.

"Well Son, believe it or not, I am a believer in the Lord Jesus Christ, as I know you are, and I choose to claim the promises God has given in His Word. "Greater is He who is in you than he who is in the world."

Chase cast a searching glance at Conyers.

"You mean to say, you think this is as much a spiritual battle as it is a physical one?" Chase asked with a look of incredulity.

Chase heard the vice president shift in his seat as he considered his words carefully.

"Yes, this very much is spiritual warfare. Satan has hated this nation from its founding because it was built upon Christian values and principles. Plus he hates us because, ever since 1948 when Israel became a nation, we have stood by her side and have been her friend. Satan hates Israel and any friend of Israel is an enemy of Satan," the vice president said with conviction.

Chase sat listening. "Do you think that the ultimate goal of Satan is the defeat of Israel?"

"Chase, that has always been Satan's goal, but the way I read my Bible, it's not gonna happen."

Chase hung up and put his phone on a universal charger. He glanced up, and took a deep breath. "Okay, here's the plan."

Unfolding a map of the area, they spent the afternoon scoping out the possible points of departure and course they would have to take, and watching a large weather system move in.

"Uh guys, if it's all the same to you, I'd rather not to take a speedboat ride up the Potomac River at midnight in a storm. I think I can be more useful as a look out for when you returned."

Nodding, Chase pulled on a jacket and turned to leave.

"Before you go Chase, you might need this," he handed him the gun Chase used to kill the sniper. It was fully loaded and the sheriff handed him several more loaded magazines.

Then he turned to Jennifer and offered her one of his, "No

thanks sheriff," she said, "I already have one, as a matter of fact, I have two and plenty of ammo." She reached inside her medical kit and drew out an Uzi and smiled.

"I am fully trained in hand to hand combat, and how to use any kind of hand gun."

# Chapter Twenty-Two

Heavy clouds blanketed the eastern seaboard as a large weather system moved in. Sweeping rain beat against the stately Naval Observatory making visibility difficult for the thin security detail surrounding it. No one heard the black hawk slip down from the sky and deliver its payload of eight highly skilled operatives.

As the lightning struck a nearby power pole, one of the members of the Delta Force cut the co-axle feeding to the surveillance cameras. The Observatory went blind.

"Sir, we have a video feed failure," said the sergeant to the watch commander, "I think it just got hit by lightning."

The watch commander crossed his arms and looked at his military issue watch. The hands were illuminated and he counted the seconds "Then in about fifteen more seconds the backup system should kick in."

It didn't. Then the power to the whole residence area went down. "Sir I can't reach the spotter on the roof, I think that we are under att—"

All at once, a flash-bang grenade exploded, stunning the security team in the control center, followed by a canister of teargas. A moment later, the room exploded into gunfire as men wearing gas-masks and night vision goggles entered and began firing. The goggles gave the commandos the advantage they needed and they fired with pin-point accuracy.

Within minutes most of the security personnel on the lower levels were neutralized and the commandos began moving about the residence ... hunting.

***

Having secured an Express Cruiser Speedboat from the Washington Harbor marina earlier in the day, Chase and Jennifer set out on their journey at what seemed the height of the storm. Jennifer proved to be an invaluable skipper as she guided the boat out into the middle of the channel and opened up the duel 350 horse power Evenrude engines. They quickly found the mouth to Rock Creek and began picking their way around the twisting channel. After an hour of fighting the swells, making switchbacks, avoiding large rocks in the water and fallen limbs, they saw a red light on the western bank just before the bridge. As they approached the dock, Chase spotted a man waving a flag.

"Head over there to that dock," he hollered over the din.

As they neared the dock the man, holding his side, reached out and guided the boat into the boat slip. "Quick," the man said, as blood seeped through his fingers. "Come with me. It may already be too late, but we must try," he said as he helped tie the boat down.

"Why? What's going on?" Jennifer asked eyeing the wounded man.

The man's shirt was soaked with rain and blood, his hair

was askew, "We've been attacked by a Delta Force team of operatives. They have cut our video feed and power and have taken out most of the security detail. The last thing I saw, was the men fanning out searching for anything that moved," the man paused and his knees buckled.

Chase grabbed him and helped him to a nearby bench. "Go on," he prompted.

The agent glanced up. "Once they have eliminated the resistance they will attempt to blow the door to the vice president's personal quarters and probably shoot him and his wife. We have got to hurry."

Chase and Jennifer checked their weapons and followed the agent to his jeep. Within minutes, they were speeding across the rain soaked lawns of Montrose and Dumbarton Park. Then they cut across Observation Circle and headed straight for the vice president's residence.

The operatives made a clean sweep of the lower levels. After killing the watch command they entered kitchen. The cooking staff proved to be more resilient than they had expected, but being out gunned and out manned, they were eventually eliminated. Then as they ascended the stairs they met with strong resistance and several of them were cut down. After several minutes of fighting, the corridors were filled with tear gas and gun smoke. The toxic mix made breathing nearly impossible.

The wounded secret service agent led them into the stately building. In the kitchen, they found all the cooking staff. As they made their way through the corridors it was not hard to imagine what had happened. The Delta operatives were totally unexpected and almost everyone was taken by surprise. Some people were shot where they stood, still others who were asleep died in their beds. It appeared that the cooks who were just starting to prepare breakfast offered some resistance but were quickly overwhelmed.

By the time the agent, Chase, and Jennifer made it up to the second and third level, most of the gunfire had ceased. The agent leading Jennifer and Chase used a mirror to peer around corners.

The first hall was clear, so they cautiously approached the next one. Suddenly, an operative stepped out of a doorway. Jennifer, with her gun at the ready, quickly turned and fired killing him instantly.

Chase gave her a shocked look.

"I hope that didn't give away our position," she whispered as she resumed her position.

The agent peeped around the next corner. Two delta operatives lay dead on the floor and further ahead lay a member of the vice president's detail. Around the next corner was the vice president's residence and this was the place where the rest of the protective detail took their stand. All of them were dead along with three Delta operatives. The remaining two were setting a C4 charge on the vice president's door and were preparing to blow it.

"Within a minute they will blow the door and be in," the

agent said whispered, "we must stop them."

One operative stood guard as the other applied the C4. As they retreated before the explosion, Jennifer and the agent stepped around the corner, took aim and fired, dropping both men.

Time ceased to matter as Chase watched the door to the vice president's living quarters explode sending shrapnel into the air. What the bullet didn't do to the agent, a piece of shrapnel did. He lay in a pool of his own blood; there was no saving him. Jennifer was blown across the room and hit the opposite wall. She lay, badly wounded.

Wishing he had his earpiece and stethoscope, Chase knew he was on his own. He leaned over Jennifer and looked into her dazed eyes, "Jennifer, can you hear me? Where are you hurt?" his throat thick with emotion.

Blinded by pain, she blinked. Her unfocused eyes stared in Chase's direction. She roused with a moaned. "I'm hurt pretty bad. Forget about me, go check on the vice president."

Chase's fingers trembled as he brushed the hair from her face. "No I can't leave you here like this," she said, then ripped a piece of his shirt and shoved it in one of the wounds. She was fading fast.

"Look, Jennifer, I need to get a medical kit from the infirmary, I'll be back in a minute. You hold on, understand?"

She nodded and returned a weak smile.

Chase, desperate to help her, dashed down the stairs.

Voices!

Chase stopped, his blood turned to ice as more killers climbed toward him. Time was running out. He scampered back up the steps. By the time he reached Jennifer, she had died. Chase didn't have the time to grieve over her; he closed her eyes and turned. The operatives were already coming around the corner. He pointed his weapon and fired, the first man fell backwards knocking the second man off balance. Then he leaped through the gaping hole left from the blast. He hit the floor and rolled behind a couch. He knew within a minute a hand grenade would be thrown in and his life would end suddenly and violently. Movement caught his eye and he turned. It was the vice president beckoning him to come into a cloak closet. Without hesitation, Chase jumped up and dove into his arms.

"Come with me quickly," the vice president said, closing the closet door. A minute later a large explosion shook the door, but it held.

Chase gave the man holding him a questioning look.

The vice president opened a secret panel and the two of them slipped behind it, and he replaced it.

"Follow me," he whispered, and began descending a flight of steps.

"Where are we going?" Chase asked as he gulped the musty air.

"This will lead to an escape tunnel built by the first Commandant of the Navy during the Civil War. It leads right out to the southern corner of the compound."

Within a minute they reached the bottom of the stairs where the vice president's wife waited, her eyes filled with anxiety.

After a brief introduction Chase's eyebrows raised questioningly. "How did you know that someone was coming to help you anyway?" Chase asked as they made their way down the dark corridor.

"I'd have to say that the Lord prompted me and I was being obedient to His voice," he said over his shoulder. "When I got to the top of the steps I heard you talking to your partner. What was her name? Jennifer?"

Chase shook his head. "Yes, Sir, her name is Jennifer, and she was a very brave woman. She will be missed," Chase said, his voice filled with emotion.

As they approached the exit of the tunnel, the vice president signaled for them to slow down and not to speak. He quietly opened the door and peeped out. It appeared to be clear. Chase, stilling his gun, held up an index finger. "I'll go first Mr. Vice President and make sure that the coast is clear."

After a quick scan of the area, Chase nodded and they charged, into the storm. They made their way in foot across the soggy lawn and reached the boat dock. Their boat bobbed violently in the storm as they untied it from its moorings. Then Chase turned the key and the duel engines came to life. He backed it out of its boat slip and carefully eased the watercraft down the river.

Lightning bolts splintered overhead illuminating the

waters as Chase retraced their course back to swelling tide of the Potomac River, its black waters threatened to swamp their boat. As they emerged into the main channel Chase saw another boat sitting out a few hundred yards from shore. He knew instinctively who they were waiting for and he jammed the throttle forward and raced out into the channel. The other boat immediately came about in hot pursuit.

To make themselves a hard target to hit, Chase kept swerving from left to right. The only hope he had was to outmaneuver and outrun them. With one hand he gripped the steering wheel and with the other, he worked the throttle varying between wide open and three-quarters depending on the how sharp a curve he made. He glanced over his shoulder and saw his pursuers gaining. White knuckled, he pushed his boat faster through the inky waters of the Potomac. Suddenly, shots rang out, pelting the waves around him.

A moment later, a large ship appeared out of the darkness. Chase spun the wheel, barely missing the vessel. In the darkness, an explosion erupted as their attackers struck the behemoth head on.

Breathing a sigh of relief, Chase slowed his boat down and cruised through the 'no wake' zone and into Tidal Basin. He found the boat slip he and Sheriff Conyers designated as their point of re-entry and landed the craft. As he turned, he noticed the vice president's wife leaning over her husband. At first, he thought they were just huddling together, but upon closer inspection, he saw blood.

"Please, he is badly wounded, I think he's been hit," she said absentmindedly.

Chase leapt to his feet and knelt next to Mrs. Randall. Blood oozed from the wounded man's abdomen.

This was the second time in the same hour that Chase wished he had his medical kit. He needed it now more than ever.

"We've got to get him to a hospital or we'll lose him," Chase said, his jaw set.

Then he grabbed the vice president by the lapels, threw him fireman style over his shoulder, and carried him up the floating dock.

Sheriff Conyers stood ready to lend a hand as soon as he was within reach.

"We need to get this man to the hospital, fast." He said between gulps of air. "If we don't hurry, we will lose the only evidence we have."

"We can't let that happen, now can we?" Conyers said as he met Chase's gaze.

The rain soaked ramp sloshed with every step, as the two men struggled to get the vice president to safety. After carefully placing the wounded man in the back seat and wrapping him in a blanket, they made sure Mrs. Randall was secured and took off in the direction of the nearest hospital.

Between dodging red lights and pedestrians, Sheriff Conyers glanced over his shoulder. "Where's Jennifer? Sheriff Conyers asked with deep concern in his voice.

Chase dropped his head and shook it slowly. "She didn't make it. She was wounded from a blast of C4 and died before I could help her. She's gone Sheriff ... I can't believe it ... she's dead."

Mrs. Randall put a tender hand on his shoulder as he sobbed. She didn't speak, but from that one act of kindness, Chase drew strength.

The moments wore on and multiplied as fatigue settled over Chase. Finally, he took a halting breath. "Thank you, Mrs. Randall. She was a brave woman. You would have liked her."

***

Using his cell phone, Sheriff Conyers call the Providence Hospital and told them the situation. Five minutes later, he rolled up to a stop in front of the emergency doors. A trauma team rushed from the emergency room and met them with a stretcher and quickly removed the stricken man from the backseat of the cruiser.

Conyers got out of his cruiser and rushed to the other side just as the trauma team was gathering around the vice president.

"This man is under police custody and is to receive a full security team STAT," the sheriff said with authority.

The emergency team responded as they were told. Within minutes, as many policemen as there were in the hospital converged in the emergency waiting area.

Conyers did some quick arithmetic. "This isn't enough

protection, we need more personnel," he said, dialing a number.

The phone rang and the precinct chief answered curtly. Conyers ignored his unfriendly greeting. "Chief, this is Conyers again, would you be so kind as to call all your buddies and have them assemble in and around the Providence Hospital. We have a very important patient in here and he doesn't want to be disturbed."

The precinct captain knew instinctively who he was referring to, and began making a few phone calls. Within an hour, the whole department gathered in the lobby of the hospital.

After a brief meeting, the men and women in uniform formed a perimeter around the hospital; some gathered on the rooftop, others took up positions in hallways, and even in the lower area where someone might slip in. soon, the hospital was completely sealed off.

Within minutes of his arrival, vice president was taken in into surgery. A team of specialists took over where the trauma doctor left off and saved the wounded man's life.

Following surgery, he was wheeled into the Recovery Room where his wife anxiously waited. For the next hour, his faithful wife sat by his bedside, praying for his recovery and for the nation.

"Doctor," Chase said, "this man is the real president of the United States."

The doctor's eyes bulged and Chase knew he had some

explaining to do "Look doc, the man who is currently running this country is a fake, a fraud, an imposter. This man, the one whose life you saved is the real James F. Randall. Now I know what you are thinking, but the only way to prove that fact is to do a DNA analysis and compare it with the current president's DNA."

The surgeon stepped back and eyed Chase suspiciously.

"Now how do you propose getting a sample of the president's DNA so that we could do the analysis?" the doctor asked, his voice sounding dubious.

Chase paced back and forth, his chin buried in his chest. After a moment of deliberation he stopped and faced the doctor. "Sir, I am an undercover agent with the FBI. I was inserted in the president's medical team for the purpose of extracting a blood sample."

"How can you prove all this?" the doctor asked eying him suspiciously.

As he spoke, Chase began pulling off his disguise. The first thing he removed was the head piece, revealing a white man. Next came the body building material, followed by his elevator shoes. When Chase finished, he stood a medium height white man, recognizable to all as the noted journalist, Chase Newton.

"Sir, my name is Chase Newton."

# Chapter Twenty-Three

**"**What do you mean you failed?" the president shouted into the phone. He scanned the Oval Office looking for something he could throw.

"You assured me that that team of operatives had an impeccable record of success and they would eliminate the vice president within minutes of taking the compound." He listened for a moment before letting out a string of expletives.

"Where is the vice president now?" he demanded. "You don't know? It's your job to know; now find him you idiot!" the president slammed down the phone, and began pacing the Oval Office, arms crossed, in deep thought.

In the shadow, stood Nguyen (Wynn) Xhu, the president's temporary Chief of Staff. She hadn't actually signed up for the role she now played, but took it when it was offered to her. As deputy to the Chief of Staff, she served Mr. Edwards. Despite his abusiveness, she served him with a meek and humble spirit. Nguyen was the exact opposite of the, now deceased, Chief of Staff in every way: from the perpetual smile, to the kindness in her light oriental voice, to the faith she had in the Lord.

Despite the thorough background check, there was one secret they had not discovered. And like an ace card, she held it close to her chest until the right moment. Now she stood before an angry president and tried her best to serve him.

Nguyen was smart, very smart. As a graduate of the University of California at Berkeley, she held an MA in Political Science and another in History. Her mother and father escaped from Vietnam. They were one of the last to be air lifted from the roof of the embassy building in Saigon when it fell into the hands of the Viet Cong on April 30th, 1975. Nguyen understood oppression, and she feared what she saw coming if this man was not stopped. She prayed for the right opportunity and for courage to act when the time came.

\*\*\*

The storm which affected the Naval Observatory had also wreaked havoc on the entire sprawling city. Power outages put a strain on the weary emergency crews, while numerous fires from lightning strikes engulfed entire city blocks.

Megan shivered in her dark cell while rescue vehicles race past the narrow window. Having taken note of it once, when the lights were on, she knew escape through it was impossible.

The uneven snoring of her captors however, gave her an idea. They had been drinking and playing poker for most of the night and now were sleeping soundly. The old rusty chair she was cuff to, also had its problems. One leg was shorter than the other and it wiggled and squeaked every time she moved. She'd figured out that if she twisted her hand just right, with a little effort, she could squeeze her small hand out of the handcuff. She moved cautiously. Once one hand was out she waited. The guard in the other room hadn't heard her movements over the sound of the storm and so she tried the other hand. After a moment of struggling, she was free.

Having memorized the layout of the building Megan tiptoed to the door and held her breath. Hers was the last room on the right. There was a front entrance and a back door. Neither was armed with an alarm, but a guard sat between both escapes. She had been praying for the Lord to deliver her and she couldn't count the times she thought about the Lord delivering Peter from prison. She knew the passage so well she nearly had it memorized. There Peter sat, chained to the wall with two armed guards standing on either side of him. Suddenly, an angel appeared in his cell and bumped him on the side and said get up, put your shoes on and let's get out of here. Peter couldn't tell if this was a dream or not, but he stood up and started walking. The chains fell off and the jail cell door swung open. The angel led the way through the first and second ward and then they came to the iron gate that led into the city. Without a squeak, it swung open and Peter marched right through as free as a bird. That's how she remembered it anyway. So she prayed that the Lord would deliver her as He did Peter. As she peeked around the corner, realized personal her only guard had fallen asleep as well. Still holding her breath, she took a step and froze. No one moved and she took a second.

Still nothing.

She tiptoed past the sleeping guards as quietly as a mouse. With trembling fingers, she gripped the handle, miraculously it turned and she pulled the door open without it making a sound. Releasing a breath, she swallowed hard and she slipped into the rainy night and was gone.

Having no idea where she was, Megan dashed down the rain slick street, her heart pounding like a stream roller. She paused briefly and squinted through the rain at a street sign. Its rusting letters held their secret and she kept running. As rain washed down her face and soaked her thin blouse, she realized how desperate her situation was. Lightning flashed temporarily blinding her, and she stumbled over a trashcan. The crash sent her tumbling into the vacant street. A chorus of dogs began to howl and she felt she had awakened the whole neighborhood. Her lungs burned and her feet began to feel like lead, but she pressed on through the night. As panic gripped her heart, she quickened her pace until she found herself running wildly through the lonely streets of the dark city. She rounded a corner and stopped to catch her breath. "Lord I don't know where I am and I need you to lead me to safety," she prayed in desperation.

After turning a few more corners and running down several streets, she began to realize where she was. It suddenly dawned on her that she was in Washington, D.C. As a teen, she'd come here many times and had seen all of the sights. Having got her bearings, she made her way to her favorite site, the Lincoln Memorial. Ever since he took that grand posture on May 30, 1922, he sat, like a gentle giant overseeing the decline of his once great nation. Megan drew strength from the sight of Mr. Lincoln, and thought of God. She saw Him through the eye of faith sitting on His throne, high and lifted up and the angels circling about crying: "Holy, Holy, Holy, Lord God Almighty." "What a privilege just to know such an almighty, prayer answering God," she mused. There she stood, soaked to the skin from rain and sweat, worshiping her Savior and God.

# Chapter Twenty-Four

" "She's what?" the president screamed into the phone. His eyes grew cold. "Are you even looking for her?" he demanded. It was going on 6:00 a.m. in the morning and no word on the whereabouts of the vice president and now this.

He was losing control. Reports were coming in that there was a press meeting scheduled for 10:00 a.m. on the steps of the Supreme Court. It was to be led by the Secretary of State Bill Ferguson with the Secretary of Defense James Higgins and Secretary of Homeland Security, Donald Appleton at his side. The news reported that several key Senators and Representatives and the Justice of District Court of Appeals in Washington, D.C. were going to join them in what appeared as a 'Tea Party' type rally. He was clearly worried. He stood motionless, staring out the window overlooking the White House lawn. "Miss Xhu," he said without turning his head. "I want you to call an emergency meeting with the Cabinet and Joint Chiefs. Also I want my Chief Legal Counsel in this room, immediately." His words came in short, angry bursts.

Nguyen bowed slightly. "Yes Sir, is there anything else?" she waited as the president continued his gaze.

"No Miss Xhu, that will be all," he answered with a

dismissive wave.

Could this be my opportunity? She wondered as she left the room. Nguyen prayed for wisdom, and she shook her head. This was not the time, she chided herself.

President Randall's eyes narrowed as he watched Miss Xhu step out of the Oval Office. When the door closed softly, he retook his seat behind the Resolute desk and reached for the telephone. He pushed a button and a man stepped into his office from another door. His shadow crossed the president's deck and he took his seat.

With eyes of fire, the man fixed his gaze on the president. "It looks like we have a big problem. All we have been working for is in jeopardy if we don't accelerate our plan. We came so close two years ago. Had we not lost the Document at the last minute, only to have it burned before our very eyes. Victory was within our grasp. We are so close to achieving our ultimate goal of world domination, and now this. It is time for phase two, don't you agree?" the stranger said through clinched teeth

President Randall nodded. He didn't like being ordered around. He didn't like being a puppet on a string, yet he complied. It was as much out of fear as it was greed for power.

"Good, then just as soon as the event takes place, you will have the support of the public to implement phase three in an accelerated pace," he said with a hiss.

Again the president He felt the fiery gaze of the dark man's eyes cutting through him, searching him, probing him.

The man rose to his feet and towered over him. "All right then, you will be hearing from us shortly." Then he stepped from the Oval Office.

A shrewd smile split President Randall's face, which transformed into a sneer, then into a cruel laugh.

# Chapter Twenty-Five

The air in the Situation Room scintillated with tension as the closed-door session between the Joint Chiefs and loyal Cabinet heads convened.

President Randall paced back and forth with a steady gait. There was a threat to his presidency and he had to act fast. He was looking to these men and women for ideas, for support.

"It is time, Mr. President," his vice president said.

Randall turned and the two men stepped from the Green Room and into the well of the Senate.

The assembly rose to their feet at the announcement by the Speaker of the House. "Ladies and Gentlemen, the President of the United States."

President Randall took his place behind the Plexiglas and faced the cameras. His jaw set, his eyes a blaze.

"Thank you, you may be seated," he said in an even tone, which belied his boiling emotions. "Ladies and gentlemen, I appreciate your coming on such short notice. In the last hour I have been given intelligence that may call us to consider raising the threat level." Heads nodded in agreement as many reviewed the prepared sheet with bullet points highlighting the latest developments.

Nguyen Xhu stepped into the room quietly and approached

the podium where the president stood. He leaned over to her, knowing already what she was about to tell him.

She whispered in his ear. "Sir, we have been attacked again." Then she handed him a sheet of paper with the details.

The president straightened as he glanced down at the paper in his hand. With as much emotion as he could generate he spoke;

"Ladies and gentlemen, I have just been informed that our nation has been attacked for the second time. If what my information is accurate, earlier this morning, the home of the incoming vice president came under attack by a group of blood thirsty militants. They killed everyone on the compound. Obviously, they were after the vice president, but thankfully, he had not moved in yet.

This coordinated with another attack which took place just moments ago. I have just been informed that someone exploded a large car bomb in the parking deck of the *New York Times* building, and completely destroyed it. The pile of debris looked like that of 9-11.

I am calling for the threat level to be raised to 'Code Red,' severe risk of terrorist attacks, and a state of emergency to be declared on a national scale. I want curfews imposed and travel restrictions extended. I want this city locked down immediately," the president said emphasizing every word.

A flurry of movement caught the president's eye as the chief legal counsel spoke up. "Sir, there are a few legal concerns that I have by imposing curfews and travel restrictions without the approval of the congress."

The president's eyes narrowed to an icy stare. "Then, let's call for both the House and the Senate to be convened immediately. Those who refuse to respond or those who oppose a unanimous decision to endorse these extreme measures obviously are infiltrators in our government. I want to know who it is that opposes these measures and have them sanctioned, impeached, and arrested for treason. I have known for some time that there are those in my administration who want to see it fail. It will not fail! We will not fail!" his phrases came in short bursts. "Anyone who opposes us will be crushed under the wheels of change."

He paused as if he'd lost his train of thought. Then, in a more conciliatory tone, he fixed his eyes on a distant horizon, and looked into the very hearts of his audience.

"Long have we waited the day when we could emerge from the shadows into the light of the national stage. Too long have our defeats plagued us, haunted us, and have dogged our heels, but no longer. Soon we will forget our sordid past, with its defeats. Imagine how different this world would be had history not recorded such defeats as the Battle of Carthage: or our defeats during the Crusader wars; the Battle of Vienna where The Ottoman Turks failed to defeat the Christians; and Battle of Waterloo where our cause was again defeated, our dream destroyed. And who could forget the French Revolution, the American Revolution, and the Battle of Yorktown? If only the tide had turned at Gettysburg, George

Washington would have been defeated. If only the course of history would have recorded a different outcome of the First World War and its sister, the Second World War. Imagine how different things would have been if only the Battle of the Bulge had not been fought, or if Stalingrad not fallen.

All of these were the work of our hands. All of these were our attempts to bring about the perfect society, and all ended in humiliation for our cause. Not this times my friends, not this time. We will rise like a great phoenix from the ashes of history and stretch our wings over the nations of the earth and they will fall at our feet. Now is the time, now is the moment."

The passion and eloquence of his speech crystallized into one mesmerizing chant. It was spellbinding, compelling, and demon possessed. Who was this man? Where did he get such power of persuasion? No one asked, no one cared, as long as their cause was accomplished. There had been other great leaders: leaders such as Caesar the Great, Herod the Great, Nero, Genghis Kohn, Napoleon, Hannibal, Saladin, Togo, Hitler, but none will be remembered for bringing in the new age. There he stood, the President of the United States of America, President James F. Randall, the man who would bring in the Age of Aquarius. The dawn of a new day was approaching and they were the makers of it. After his captivating speech, assembly rose to give his a standing ovation.

# Chapter Twenty-Six

hase, Sheriff Conyers, and the entire hospital staff of Providence Hospital stood in silent shock as they watched news of the explosion unfold. The video footage of the devastation showed how complete the destruction of *The New York Times* building was. Within minutes of the blast, Police and Fire and Rescue poured into the area, trying to save the victims and rescue the dying. Ambulances filled the streets; Doctors and nurses from the surrounding medical facilities rushed to the scene. It was September 11th, 2001 all over again.

Medical teams from Providence Hospital began to assemble in response to the incoming trauma victims. The chief of security had already decided, that despite the risk posed to the vice president, he couldn't turn away the many injured he expected to arrive. To insure the vice president's safety, he had him moved into the psychiatric ward and placed armed guards at every point of entry. Within minutes, the ambulances began to arrive.

Tears streamed down Chase's face as he stood and watched the column of smoke rise heavenward and defuse into the skyline. To him, this was the memorial honoring the final sacrifice of his friends and colleagues. He took a glance at the wall clock. It was 8:00 in the morning and the building was filled with secretaries, reporters, editors, and proofreaders. The printing presses would have been running, and delivery trucks would have been sitting at the ready to receive the latest edition. But rather than report the news, the New York Times became the news.

Chase flopped heavily into a hospital chair and sobbed. Everyone he held dear was dead, dying, or soon to be. First it was Glenn Tibbits, the man that stood courageously against the evils of his day. Then it was Jennifer, a woman of character and courage. Never once did she lead him on or act in a provocative way. She was truly a virtuous woman, a woman of God. And now it was his dear friend Stan Berkowitz. Stan drove him to be the best he could be and then some. How he missed him already! As far as he knew, within the next hour, his lovely wife, Megan, would be dead and he was powerless to stop it. How could he get the results of the two DNA tests into the hands of the largest newspaper in the world when its hub lay in ashes?

Brokenhearted, Chase began to cry out to God. He was at the end of his rope. The last night of decent sleep was on the plane. By now he had been awake for nearly twenty-four hours. Mentally and physically exhausted, his faith wavered.

"God, I know that you said 'all things work together for good to them that love you, to them who are called according to your purposes,' but right now I don't see any good coming out of this. All my friends have been killed, and my wife as far as I know may already be dead too. It looks like the Devil is about to score a big one this time, and I am helpless to stop him." As Chase sat in the waiting room, the Lord's voice echoed in his ear. It was a verse in I Kings 19:18 his pastor preached on the previous Sunday. "Yet I have left me seven thousand in Israel, all the knees which have not bowed unto Baal, and every mouth which hath not kissed him."

Chase took in a halting breath and let it out slowly. "That was exactly what I needed to hear," he said to himself. He took courage knowing that there were still many who had not surrendered to the whims of societal evolution. While he waited for direction, he allowed his mind to relax and drifted off to sleep.

# Chapter Twenty-Seven

An hour after falling asleep, Chase jolted to life. Looking around, he saw a crowd of doctors, nurses and family members gathered in front of a television. Pushing himself up, he wobbled, then caught himself on the back of a chair. He leaned heavily on it until his mind cleared. When it did, he staggered to the group of people staring at the television. An announcer's voice echoed throughout the waiting room as the hastily convened meeting between both Houses of Congress was called to order.

Chase's heart quickened as he watched the president, flanked by the people who plotted against his nation, take his place behind the podium.

"My fellow Americans, today our homeland has been struck again by tragedy. Forces within our borders who oppose this administration and who have worked long and hard to see it fail have lashed out against us. These are the same people who claim to love and pray for our country; who wave the American flag the most vigorously, who fill the airwaves with the constant rants against the perceived shortcomings of this government, this administration. They are the ones who oppose free speech, who oppose the rights of a woman to choose. Who stand against the rights of our elderly to choose when and how they will die? They are not the real Americans. They are not the true patriots. They seek to divide us over trivial things such as religion, creation versus evolution, abortion rights versus the rights of the mother, conservative versus liberal, and the list goes on and on. They claim that if you don't agree with them you are un-American. Well I'm an American, and I don't agree with them. As a matter of fact, the vast majority of Americans don't agree with them, and so what does that make us? Traitors? No, my friends, I submit to you that they who would wish us failure are the ones who are the traitors of America.

So today, I am submitting to the congress new legislation that will weed out those who would seek our defeat and bring them to justice. In essence, this new legislation will require everyone to obtain a 'Citizenship of the World' card. This card, which will have a PIC, a Personal Information Chip can be obtained by swearing allegiance to the United States of the World. With this card, you will be given all the rights offered to you as an American citizen. You will be allowed to buy and sell and participate in commerce as you always have. You will be allowed to conduct your affairs just as you always have, only on a grander scale because you will be a citizen of a much larger family, the family of the world. If you refuse to swear allegiance to the United States of the World, you will soon run out of money, your bank accounts and all assets will be frozen, your driver's licenses will no longer be valid, your credit cards will not be accepted. You will be hunted down, imprisoned, tried for treason, and shot. Also, as a part of this sweeping new legislation we are breaking off all diplomatic ties with the State of Israel. I have instructed the Ambassador to Israel to return to the United States without delay. I have been given evidence, irrefutable proof that it was members of the Mossad, Israel's elite delta force, who perpetrated this unprovoked attack upon this nation.

Far too long has the Israeli government provoked their peace loving neighbors with their inflammatory rhetoric. Far too long have they flaunted their very existence in the faces of our friends, the Palestinians, the Syrians, and our friends the Iraqis, and have built settlements in the occupied lands which do not belong to them. This must stop!"

He interrupted his diatribe for a moment to allow his teleprompter to advance before continuing.

"Effective immediately we are calling for the withdrawal of all Israeli military and civilian personnel from the Golan Heights, from the West Bank, and from the occupied areas. Also, we are demanding reparations be made to those affected by their senseless and willful disobedience to World Law. If Israel refuses to comply within the next 48 hours, I am authorizing our military leadership to begin to draw up plans that would include the neighboring countries of the State of Israel to join us in enforcing World Law."

"I also have signed into law a national curfew and declared a state of emergency. This will effectively stop all interstate commerce and travel. This state of emergency will only be lifted when the population comes into compliance with the new standing law of the land."

Again he paused and let the spontaneous applause subside. "Now I know that these measures that I have taken may seem harsh, and for the short-term they may even be painful, but in the long run they will pay great dividends. When all of these malcontents are removed from our midst, we will then have the perfect society that we all have longed for. This perfect society will be one that allows you to become whatever and whoever you long to be. To express yourself in any way you think best without the old Victorian values that have been imposed upon us, we will finally throw off the restraints, the chains, and the shackles that have held us back. We will truly be a free society."

As he concluded his comments, the whole congress stood to its feet in thunderous applause. President Randall stood, basking in his glory. "I have opposed the God of Heaven and have gotten away with it." He muttered as he stepped off of the platform: "What power, with the stroke of the pen it's the law of the land. Indeed the pen is mightier than the sword, especially when I am holding the pen."

He had won.

# Chapter Twenty-Eight

After giving his speech, President Randall returned to the Oval Office, where Miss Xhu waited. She handed him his usual cup of hot tea with a weak smile. It was his tradition to enjoy the hot brew to sooth his dry after every speech.

"Thank you Miss Xhu that will be all," he said, dismissively.

She bowed politely and started to back away. "One more thing, Mr. President," she said, her eyes searching the floor.

His eyes narrowed and he turned impatiently. "What is it Miss Xhu?"

She hesitated knowing the kind of response she would get. "It's the Internet. It has gotten a hold of some news about a conspiracy theory and there are people converging on Washington from all over the country. As we speak there is a gathering of Senators, Members of the House of Representatives and even some from your Cabinet on the steps of the Supreme Court. They are standing in opposition to the measures you have just proposed. There is a press conference scheduled for 2 o'clock this afternoon."

The president blistered the air with a string of expletives, which cursed her Lord and Savior. Righteous indignation swelled in her heart. She bit her lip and prayed. Fists in tight balls, she retraced her steps.

As the door closed, President Randall plopped down behind the Resolute desk, his jaw set, his eyes a blaze with unchecked anger. He took a sip of tea and picked up the phone. "Get me the National Guard," he demanded, then slammed down the phone.

Within a minute the commander of the Washington, D.C. brigade of the National Guard picked up the phone.

President Randall leaned into the phone and spoke through clinched teeth. "Get down here and restore order. Anyone who resists you, arrest them. If they get out of hand, use whatever force you deem necessary to quash this rebellion."

"Yes, Sir." Then the connection ended.

Randall fingered the phone cable. Had this been Gay Pride week, I would have done nothing; but this, this threatened all I've worked for, all I've dreamed for. His anger was palpable as he stepped into the anteroom off from the Oval Office.

Within an hour tanks and armored personnel carriers began to converge on the chanting, singing, praying masses. Undeterred by the threatening show of force, the courageous people of America stood their ground.

The tea Nguyen prepared for the president was an old recipe made from leaves and herbs she'd recently received from Vietnam. As he sipped his tea, he suddenly sat upright. A sharp pain cut through his chest like a knife and he gasped for breath. Sweat beaded on his brow and he stood, leaning heavily on the desk. He loosened his collar and tried to breath but his throat constricted. With his heart racing, he staggered a few steps and collapsed on the floor of the anteroom.

The moment his body fell to the floor, he heard a voice. It wasn't the voice of Miss Xhu. Neither was it his personal secretary. It was the voice of Him who holds the universe in His hand. "You have been weighed in the balances and have been found wanting ... this day your soul is required of you." In a moment President Randall stood before the Sovereign God of the universe.

By the time they found the president's body, Nguyen Xhu had left the premises.

Immediately upon hearing the president's address to the nation, it was broadcast to the world. Nations began moving men and material into position in an effort to force the Israeli government to comply with World Law. The madman of Iraq readied his nuclear missile launchers. The moment he had been praying to Allah for had finally come. He would personally lead his forces across the Syrian Desert and into the land of Israel. The Russian government began transporting vast amounts of land forces through Georgia, having virtually stripped the tiny nation of any military resistance on August 8, 2008. The Palestinian blockade was penetrated and fresh arms began to pour into the Gaza Strip. Israel who was already surrounded with hostile nations, now found herself drifting alone in an angry Arab sea, without a friend in the world.

# Chapter Twenty-Nine

Sirens from passing ambulances and fire trucks cut through the thick morning air jolting Megan from her sleep. As her mind began to clear, Megan sneezed as the smoke-filled air assaulted her nostrils. Where am I? And what am I doing here in the Lincoln Memorial? The question danced on the fringes of her mind, and she recounted the previous night. She'd escaped from her abductors and wandered through the streets of Washington, D.C. until finding the Lincoln Memorial. It was here, within the safety of this gentle giant, spent the night. But why the sirens, and where is the smoke and debris coming from?

Fearful, and yet inquisitive, Megan stood and began making walking in the direction of the smoke. The closer she got, the more she recognized the area. It was downtown Washington, D.C. and this was the area her husband worked. She saw the twisted street sign bearing the name G Street. Were it not for the smoke she could have seen the White House. The closer she got to the center of the activity the more Fire and Emergency vehicles she encountered, the thicker the smoke became and the more she recognized the area. It suddenly dawned on her that the source of the smoke and debris was her husband's office building ... *The New York*

*Times* building or what was left of it.

Megan's pulse quickened and her throat closed at the thought of her husband and his colleagues being incinerated in that firestorm. Warmth streamed down her face as she thought about losing her husband without having one last opportunity to say, "I love you."

Suddenly, Megan felt vulnerable and exposed. Although there were hundreds of people all around her, she stood in the midst of the chaos and for the first time in her life felt all alone.

\*\*\*

With the announcement of a state of emergency being declared and a curfew being imposed, the American people were thrown into a state of confusion. Employees didn't know if they should leave their place of work and get home or stay and finish out the day. Shop owners didn't know if they should close for the day or try to maintain the work schedule. In many cities, unruly mobs flooded the grocery stores and bought or stole all that was on the shelves. Within the day, grocery stores closed their doors and boarded up their windows. In many cases there was no hope of reopening them because no shipments would be permitted to enter the state to resupply them.

Street gangs began roaming the city streets plundering and looting as they went. It was not safe to walk the streets as the unsuspecting fell into their clutches.

As she stood in the middle of the street Megan suddenly

realized the danger she was in. It would only be a matter of time before a marauding gang would catch her, or the police would arrest her for violating curfew, or worse, her abductors would find her. But her feet were anchored to the concrete and she stood staring, hoping and praying she'd awake and find this an awful nightmare … it wasn't.

***

Throughout the day, television crews and radio announcers scoured the area covering the mayhem. As one particular cameraman panned the area for background footage, he unknowingly caught Megan in his lens. Immediately, her face was slashed across the nation in plain sight for all to see. What started as a simple act by the cameraman developed into a life and death race between two men.

"Get me down town," The Dean demanded, and he and his men piled into a car and sped in the direction of the New York Times.

Chase stared at the television screen, his mouth gaped open. Was that Megan? His mind screamed. What is she doing down there?

Grabbing the sheriff by the shoulder, he shook him from his map. Sheriff, wake up."

He groaned and cracked an eye. "Why? What's going on?" His voice was thick, groggy.

"Sheriff, I just saw Megan on TV. She'd down town right across from the *New York Times*."

Knowing the danger she was in, the sheriff sprang to his

feet and jogged after Chase. They jumped into his police cruiser and squealed rubber.

As they weaved between slow moving cars, Chase's heart pounded, and he prayed he could get to her before her captors did.

Blocks away and coming from the opposite direction, The Dean's eyes burned with unchecked hate as he thought of the last time his cause was thwarted by Megan and Chase.

Through the smoke and haze the figure of a man emerged behind Megan, "Ma'am, would you mind coming with me," said a rather well dressed gentleman. The bulge under his tailored suit told her that he was carrying a weapon and that it probably would not be a good time to for her to run.

Megan felt the color drain from her face. "Why? Where are you taking me?" she asked, her eyes widening.

Ignoring the question, the man quietly nodded in the direction of the car.

Megan's legs turned to water, as a wave of panic swept over her. Her mind raced in circles and she caught herself not breathing. She searched the eyes of the well-dressed man. Rather than seeing malice, she saw warmth, a tenderness lacking in the eyes of the Dean and his associates. Meekly, she took a step and the man gave her a soft smile. Who was he? And what did he want? He wasn't one of the thugs who had been holding me captive, and he clearly wasn't an official policeman.

Without speaking guided her to a waiting car, opened the

front passenger door and nodded to her to get in. Megan hesitated, then got in. He gently closed the door and stepped around to the driver's side.

He got in, started the car and gradually pulled away from the curb. His movements were smooth and professional and Megan began to breathe again.

As the sleek black car swerved around the corner, the driver broke the tense moment. "Ma'am, I am one of the vice president's security detail," he said quietly. He asked me to escort you to a safe house where we can offer you protection and care for your immediate needs. Would you permit us to do that?"

Megan's eyes bulged, her hand covering her gaping mouth. "How did you find me? And what's the vice president this got to do with? Her mind swirled like a dust-devil.

His answer echoed hollow as she watched a black Volvo turn the corner. Megan recognized the driver as being one of the men who had held her captive.

# Chapter Thirty

T he Volvo came to an abrupt stop and two men jumped out and raced to the intersection ... they found the corner vacant. "Go back and circle the block. She'd got to be here," The Dean hollered to his driver. The man disappeared in the smoke, leaving The Dean alone to search for his prey.

A billow of smoke drifted across the intersection obscuring the emergency and police cruisers, including one with out of state plates.

Through the haze, the silhouette of a disorientated man appeared on the corner. It was obvious to The Dean, the man was unaware of his presence or the danger he was in. The advantage was clearly his as he approached the young man from the back. He would have to act quickly, but with any luck, he could kill Chase before he did any more damage.

Cautiously, The Dean circled around to his left and allowed a wisp of smoke to come between him and his prey. Although he didn't usually carry a weapon, since he'd gotten into the abduction business, he was never without one. As he approached the young man he drew his gun, and pointed it at the man's head.

"Well, Mr. Newton, we finally meet. Put your hands up

and turn around slowly," he said with a sneer.

The man slowly raised his arms to the air and turned revealing a frightened elderly man in his fifties. His wide eyes were enlarged by his rimless glasses as he stared at the weapon.

The Dean swallowed hard, his mouth turned to cotton as it occurred to him that it wasn't Chase Newton but rather, an innocent bystander. Staring into the frightened man's eyes of, he saw fear, fear of the unknown, the fear of death, and he drank in his fear like a thirsty man. Should I continue to play out the game? Should I shoot the man where it stands? The Dean's finger twitched.

Again a cloud of smoke swept across the street corner and enshrouded the two men. It was as if the world closed its eyes to any more death and destruction.

The shape of a man appeared in the haze and a shot rang out. The Dean stood, holding his weapon, his eyes wide with shock. He staggered backward trying to keep his equilibrium. Turning, he raised his gun with his right hand while clutching his chest. Blood seeped between his fingers and he fired wildly. Another shot rang out and struck him with deadly force. His body fell to the ground with a sickening thud. A labored breath escaped his lungs as a pool of crimson ran down the sidewalk and into the gutter.

Rarely had Sheriff Conyers seen such shock and disbelief on another man's face than on The Dean's. His report would state he saw a man attempting to rob an innocent bystander. He lowered his sidearm and returned it to its holster.

Within seconds, a Television crew and a number of police officers assembled at the scene. Because of his uniform and badge, there were few questions and soon Sheriff Conyers returned to his vehicle, only to find it empty. "Chase, where'd ya go?" He called through the haze. *Why would he go wandering off with danger all around him?*

A search of the area uncovered no clue as to the whereabouts of his friend. Frantically, he dialed Chase's cellphone ... he got no answer. All attempts at locating Chase proved to be fruitless. Chase simply had vanished into thin air.

# Chapter Thirty-One

"Stop the car," Megan demanded, as the driver rounded the corner.

The driver eased up on the accelerator and turned.

"Sir, please. Back up, I think I saw something important."

At her direction, her driver made a U-turn and came back. A police cruiser with its door standing open sat, parked along the curb. The vice president's body guard drove up to it, and rolled down his window. Inside the cruiser sat Chase looking rather bewildered. Recognizing him, he got out and approached the side of the car. "Sir, I think you need to come with me."

Chase stared at the figure looming over him in disbelief. Suddenly, it dawned on him, he must be one of the vice president's body guards. Chase stood and followed the man around to the passenger side and got in. Megan threw her slender arms around his neck. "Chase," she cried and buried her head in his shoulder. Another cloud of smoke drifted across the intersection and the car disappeared.

"Oh Chase, I've been so worried about you," she said, her throat closing with emotion.

The warmth of Megan's trembling body radiated through his Chase thin shirt as he held her close. "It's all right, I'm here now. You're safe," he said and kissed away her tears.

As the driver maneuvered through the menagerie of abandoned cars, he speed dialed his boss' number.

"Yes, Sir, I got her and a bonus ..."

Chase and Megan listened to the one sided conversation. "No, Sir, not The Dean, but it is someone I'm sure you will be glad to meet ..." he paused for new instructions. "The Providence Hospital?" the driver paused a moment. "Yes, Sir, I'll come as quickly as I can," he said as he tapped his earpiece, ending the conversation. Then he changed lanes and took the highway leading to the hospital.

Megan turned to Chase with a confused look on her face. He reached over and brushed the hair from her eyes. "You look like you've been through a lot," eying her disheveled hair and rumpled clothes.

"That evil man made me call you, and wouldn't let me talk. What did he want?"

Chase placed an index finger over her lips with a tender smile. "It was—"

"Sir, Ma'am," said the driver interrupted, as he peered into the rearview mirror. "I just got a call from the vice president. He has asked me to return to Providence Hospital. I hope you don't mind."

Megan placed her hand on Chase's arm and clutched his shirtsleeve. "Chase, what is going on? I don't understand," she said, her voice turning shaky.

"M," Chase tried to keep his voice calm. "You wouldn't

believe it, but the last ten days our nation has been under attack and you were in the very eye of the storm."

"I was?" her eyes widened. "Who were those men that abducted me and why did they want you?"

Chase looked deeply into her eyes and considered his answer. He knew the pain it would cause her to tell her about the death of Glenn and Jennifer. He also knew he'd eventually have to tell her, but not then. Too much hung in the balance.

"What does the vice president have to do with all this?" the tension in her voice brought him to his senses, begging an answer.

The memories of the past days chaffed at his mind. He didn't know where to begin and so he simply kissed her. "You need to trust me, M. we've not out of the woods yet."

Twenty minutes later they were exiting the freeway. As they approached the hospital the security detail opened the parking gate and let the car pass through. Upon arriving, they made their way up to the floor where the vice president awaited them. Still shaky, he pushed himself to his feet, and extended his hand.

"Mr. and Mrs. Newton, it is so good to see you," the vice president said sincerely.

Chase gripped his hand firmly and looked him in the eyes. "It's good to see you, Mr. Vice President. You look much better than the last time we met."

Megan's eyes widened as he gave her a fatherly hug. "I am so sorry that you were dragged into this mess. I can't imagine what you must have gone through, young lady. I must hear all about it in time." Then, looking at Chase he continued, "I owe you my life Chase, and the country owes you a huge debt of gratitude."

"Well it may be too soon to start popping open the champagne, Mr. Vice President. We still have a very dangerous situation to defuse."

With a nod, the vice president took his seat and an orderly wheeled his to a makeshift desk. "Yes, President Randall, or whoever he is, has called out the National Guard," he said, winching from a cough.

"Level with us, are you going to be all right?"

A wry smile parted the man's lips. "The doctors say I'll make a full recovery from my wounds. They also inform me that my wound is in the exact location as that of the president's. If it weren't for the fact that I was also wearing protective body armor, that bullet would have killed me, but by God's grace it didn't. That's got me thinking ..."

For the next thirty minutes he mapped out a new strategy for saving the nation, but the clock was ticking.

# Chapter Thirty-Two

A long with the new order being imposed upon society, came new restrictions. Not only were there travel restrictions, but also restrictions of the press and free speech. Television stations and radio stations fell under new and very restrictive rules. Talk show hosts were the first to feel the muzzle.

Within the hour of the news conference, special police units stormed radio stations and locked them down. Many of the popular talk show hosts who opposed the restriction were arrested and frog marched to jail before the stations could mount a counter attack. However, the Internet was alive and well. It was there the counter attack began.

Hours earlier, Chase had opened up Glenn's laptop and logged on to the Internet. He found a string connecting to the now infamous, 'WikiLeaks,' and downloaded all the files. Within minutes, the information went viral. Bloggers picked up the information, and spread the information even further. By 9:00 a.m. everyone who had access to a computer knew of the conspiracy in our government. By 10:00 a.m. cars, buses, RV campers filled with loyal, red-blooded Americans descended upon the nation's capital. They filled the Mall and lapsed over into the streets. Soon the streets around the Capital and White House were inundated with angry Americans. The thin wall of barriers, hastily put in place National Guard and police, soon gave as the massive crowds surged into the restricted areas.

***

In the congress, the opponents of the president's mandates were easily defeated and the new bill was quickly enacted. The proponents of the Constitution were immediately labeled as dissidents and troublemakers. Desperate to save their beleaguered nation, the loyalists took one last stand and called for a two o'clock press conference on the steps of the Supreme Court.

Surrounded by a chorus of peaceful demonstrators and antagonistic press, the courageous Senators, Representatives, and Cabinet Heads stood shoulder to shoulder in the spotlight. Each one in turn stood in front of the microphone and read from Glenn Tibbit's computer files. Others read from the Constitution and pointed out the places where the president and the out-of-control Congress had overstepped its boundaries. Together, they demanded the impeachment of the president and for the members of his cabinet to step down. With this new information, they called for their colleagues in the Congress to reassess their support of the state of emergency and called for the lifting of the curfew and sanctions against Israel.

As Secretary of State, Bill Ferguson spoke before a mesmerized audience, a black limousine with United States flags on its front fenders slowly pushed its way through the throng. It was flanked by an army of secret service agents and the crowd reluctantly parted letting the oversized Cadillac through. The presidential limousine continued to make its way through the mass of people until it stopped directly in front of the podium. Secret agents stepped to the side of the automobile and opened the door. The image of the President of the United States of America emerged from the shadow of the vehicle. He stood erect and straightened his tie as he scanned the unfriendly crowd. He frowned back at their angry faces. Immediately, the crowd became restless and began to 'boo' at him.

The president, impervious to their reaction, stepped up to the speaker, "Sir, may I have a word with the American people?"

The ashen faced Secretary of State swallowed hard and yielded the floor to his commander in chief.

The president stepped and gave the Secretary of State room to move, then took his place behind the podium. Before speaking, he surveyed the masses, his dark eyes taking in the fearful glare of the assembly. Then, in a clear voice of authority he began to address the people.

"Ladies and gentlemen, citizens of this great land," the president said. "Within the last hour I have been informed that those whom I have trusted to keep me informed with the most accurate and honest information have been deceiving me." He paused and let the suspense build.

"But since I am the president, I take full responsibility for my actions. I acted upon misleading, and fallacious information, and so, effective immediately, I am rescinding my call for a state of emergency and I am lifting the curfew. Within the hour, I will be calling my dear friend, the prime minister of Israel, and make a full apology for maligning his character and motives. I am prepared to send whatever help our friends in the Israeli Defense Force might have to stand against the aggressors surrounding them. I am calling for Russia and the Iraqis to cease and desist all military actions against our friend, Israel. To proceed against this peace loving nation will be the same as attacking our land. As one of our flags of history once said, 'Don't Tread On Me.'" The president paused and let the tentative applause subside and then continued.

"The PIC, or Personnel Information Chip, as I have been informed, is an intrusion into the privacy of the American people and I am calling for an immediate recall of this device. I am also appointing a Blue Ribbon Committee to investigate those in my administration who have been working behind my back to bring about the demise of this great land. And so, my fellow Americans, breathe the fresh air of freedom."

To his delight, the audience who had booed moments earlier now cheered him. How easily swayed these people are. They are like sheep having no shepherd, he mused.

"I will be relentless in my pursuit of the truth and ferret out every traitor to the Constitution, so help me God," he said vehemently.

Again the audience cheered and spontaneously broke out singing "God Bless America." The president paused while the audience cheered, and then continued.

"I will also submit to the congress an executive order demanding the immediate removal of the current vice president and will appoint my good friend, and colleague Bill Ferguson, The Secretary of State, as my acting vice president until the Congress approves him. Bill's reaction to such an announcement was palpable as he stood mouth gaped open.

As all of you know, there have been rumors of a great conspiracy, something about DNA and me not being who they say I am. Well, let me assure you, I am President James F. Randall, the real James F. Randall and to prove it, I am calling for Dr. Cleve Newberry the man who is responsible for saving my life, to step to the podium."

Movement stirred in the back of the crowd and as a well-built black man, dressed in a medical overcoat stepped out and approached the platform followed by a nurse.

The president greeted them warmly with a handshake. "Sir, could you state your name and occupation for the press."

He stepped closer to the microphone and addressed the audience. "Good afternoon, I am Dr. Cleve Newberry and I am the doctor who treated the president in Mogadishu when he initially received his injury. I was there to assist him on Air Force One and to see that he was stable before returning to the scene of the ambush and rescuing the remaining security detail, including my nurse assistant Miss Hodges. I stand here today and can confirm that this man is indeed James F. Randall, the President of the United States. I also am holding in my hand a copy of the DNA results proving that he is who he claims to be." He straightened and raised the evidence up for all to see.

As the president retook his position behind the microphone he continued to address the people of America by reciting the Preamble to the Constitution by memory

Chase and Megan, flanked by Sheriff Conyers and the secret service agent, stood and cheered, hugged and waved American flags. But it didn't go unnoticed by Chase that as the president spoke; he lightly touched the top of the podium with the tips of his fingers.

# Epilogue

Thank you for taking the time to read Stranger in the White House. When I set out to write this novel, I did not want to simply write a commentary on today's political climate. But I did want to communicate the gospel couched in an exciting, action-packed story with a plausible scenario. There are at least two clear presentations of the gospel message: One given by the pastor at Glenn's funeral, and the other one was when our friend the sheriff told Chase his testimony. If, as a part of reading this, you sensed your need to trust Christ and did so, let me celebrate with you. You can do so by sending an e-mail to me at authorbryanpowell@reagan.com.

## The Chase Newton Series (Formerly the Stranger Series)
### *by Bryan M. Powell*

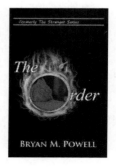

### The Order
Follow investigative reporter Chase Newton as he goes undercover in search of the truth. What he finds puts him and those he cares for in mortal danger. Fast-paced and high- energy describes this first of three mystery and action thrillers.

### The Oath
The president and vice president have been attacked. The vice president survived, but he is a hunted man. The man who was sworn in is an impostor and Chase must get a DNA from him to prove who the real president is.

### The Outsider
After a thousand years of peace, the world is suddenly thrown into chaos as Satan is loosed from his prison. These action-packed stories will hold you breathless and capture your imagination until the exciting conclusion.

## The Jared Russell Series
*by Bryan M. Powell*

**Sisters of the Veil**
Jared Russell, a former Marine turned architect, must navigate the minefield of hatred and prejudice to find the meaning of love and forgiveness.
**ISBN - 978151057994**

**Power Play - #8 on Amazon Political Fiction**
Jared and Fatemah Russell go to Beirut, Lebanon, to establish the Harbor House, a refuge for converted Muslims and find themselves caught in a Middle East conflict of global proportions.
**ISBN – 9781511402750**

**The Final Countdown – #25 on Amazon**
The clock is ticking and Jared once again finds himself battling against forces beyond his control. Can he and his friends unravel the mystery in time to stop two radical Muslims from perpetrating a horrible crime against our country?
**ISBN – 978153297825**

*Bryan M. Powell*

**Christian Fantasy Series**
*by Bryan M. Powell*

**The Witch and the Wise Men**
An ancient medallion is discovered,
An evil spirit is awakened,
A witch's curse is broken …
And the wise men of Bethlehem are called upon to
face the ultimate evil.

**The Lost Medallion**
Beneath the Hill of Endor is a Temple
Inside the Temple is a Chamber,
Inside the Chamber is a door,
Behind the door … the abyss.
And the key to the door is the witch's medallion.

**Non-Fiction Series**
*by Bryan M. Powell*

**Seeing Jesus a Three Dimensional Look at Worship**
Seeing Jesus is a thought provoking and compelling expose' on what is true worship. ISBN -9781511540582

**Show Us the Father**
A thirty-day devotional showing how Jesus demonstrated His Father's character and qualities.
ISBN -9781517633905

**Faith, Family, and a Lot of Hard Work**
Born the year the Stock-Market crashed, Mr. Gillis grew up in South Georgia with a 3rd grade education. After being challenged to get the best job in the company, he worked hard and got a degree from the University of Georgia and Moody Bible Institute in Finance. By mid-life, he owed 14 companies. ISBN -9781467580182

## *About the Author*

Novelist Bryan M. Powell is the author of 8 Christian Fiction novels, 2 Inspirational Books and 1 Memoir he co-authored. Working within a Christian ministry for over forty-two years, Bryan is uniquely qualified to write about Christian topics. His novels have been published by Tate Publishing, Lightening Source, Create Space, Kindle Direct Publishing and Vabella Publishing. His latest novel, The Witch and the Wise Men, held the #23 slot on Amazon's best seller's list.

In addition to his novels, Bryan's short stories and other works appeared in *The North Georgia Writer* (PCWG's publication), *Relief Notes* (A Christian Authors Guild's book, released in 2014), and in the *Georgia Backroads* magazine.

Bryan is a member of the following organizations: American Christian Fiction Writers (ACFW), The Christian Author's Guild (President, 2016), The Paulding County Writers' Guild (PCWG), and the local chapter of ACFW, the New Life Writers Group.

www.facebook.com/authorbryanpowell
www.authorbryanpowell.wordpress.com

Made in the USA
Columbia, SC
09 February 2020